Riku Can't Be a Goddess

Riku Can't Be a Goddess

WRITTEN BY

Kumi Tamaru

Seven Seas Entertainment

Seven Seas press and purchase enquiries can be sent to
Marketing Manager Lauren Hill at press@gomanga.com.
Information regarding the distribution and purchase of
digital editions is available from Digital Manager CK Russell
at digital@gomanga.com.

Follow Seven Seas Entertainment online at
sevenseasentertainment.com.

TRANSLATION: Sarah Burch
ADAPTATION: Kat Adler
COVER DESIGN: H. Qi
INTERIOR LAYOUT & DESIGN: Clay Gardner
COPY EDITOR: Mark DeJoy
PROOFREADER: Vivica Caligari
EDITOR: Laurel Ashgrove
PREPRESS TECHNICIAN: Melanie Ujimori, Jules Valera
MANAGING EDITOR: Alyssa Scavetta
EDITOR-IN-CHIEF: Julie Davis
PUBLISHER: Lianne Sentar
VICE PRESIDENT: Adam Arnold
PRESIDENT: Jason DeAngelis

ISBN: 979-8-88843-763-6
Printed in Canada
First Printing: July 2024
10 9 8 7 6 5 4 3 2 1

Table of Contents

PART 1
The Beautiful Bombshell

Riku Can't Be a Goddess

"I'M DONE. You can look now, Ichika."

I followed the sweet yet raspy voice's instructions and opened my eyes.

He giggled happily, small puffs of his breath tickling the tip of my nose. "I knew buying this mascara was the right choice! That cool eye shadow shade I chose looks fabulous. And I managed to draw sleek lines with that eyeliner." He smiled with satisfaction as he admired his creation—my face—from very close proximity. "You're so cute, Ichika!"

His almond-shaped eyes were well-defined, with smoldering pupils, and his lips were glossy with a scarlet sheen. There was something inherently sexy about the way he stroked the raven-colored hair that fell around his chest as he handed me the mirror. As he sat with his long legs crossed, his mere presence made me feel like the room could burst gloriously into bloom at any moment.

"I did a good job today, huh?"

"Of course you did. It's you, Riku."

As I praised his makeup skills, Riku let out a feminine giggle. His stylish posture was the result of research into how to appear more delicate. He wore a tight dress that exposed his long, pale limbs, and there wasn't a hint of pudginess to his slender frame.

"I'm so jealous, Ichika. Whatever makeup or clothes I choose look good on you."

He laid out his new cosmetics, then tried them on my face one by one.

"You'll be all done once I put on this gloss," he drawled in a husky voice so sweet it sent shivers down my spine.

Once he'd applied an ample amount of cherry-scented gloss to my lips, the look was complete. He stared at me again; his makeup skills had accentuated both the intensity of his eyes, and his lips' seductive curl.

Riku and I were childhood friends. I couldn't recall a time when he hadn't been in my life. He was stunningly beautiful, and there was something alluring about every tiny movement he made. It just so happened that his hobby was dolling me up as girlishly as possible—that, and dressing as a woman himself.

"You'll like this gloss. It isn't highly pigmented, so you could even wear it to school."

Riku giggled again as he placed the tube in my hand with a coquettish flourish. His gesture stretched the neckline of his dress slightly, showing off the pale skin on his chest. The sight made my heart skip a beat, despite knowing he was as flat as board underneath. There was no denying that he was a boy.

Riku spent every day after school in my room. He'd taken up a whole section with his makeup collection and wardrobe; he loved using those to dress us both up to his heart's content.

He was always on top of the latest trends thanks to his constant research through reading magazines and watching videos online. Using me as his real-life practice mannequin, he'd cultivated makeup techniques that could rival most girls'.

That wasn't just due to his technical skills, either. Riku could utilize his androgynous looks in a way that somehow outdid female classmates. His long, straight wig exuded a glamorous aura, yet the way the corners of his eyes crinkled when he smiled was the epitome of cuteness. He could pick up his favorite teddy bear and hold it to the tip of his nose with the same innocent charm as any little girl.

With each new gesture and expression, he became more and more fascinating. Although we saw each other daily, I never got tired of watching him.

"Must be nice to be a girl," Riku mused. "They can be totally gorgeous with just a little effort."

"Is that sarcasm I detect?"

Riku giggled as he sat on the bed. "You noticed? Thanks."

Then, as if it were the most natural thing in the world, he pulled me into his lap.

"Ichika, can I touch you?" he whispered.

The voice that tickled my ears was so sweet, I thought I might melt into a puddle on the spot. I barely had time to say "Okay..." before Riku slid his hand inside my top.

He started by running his fingers down my side, over my camisole, and drawing a circle around my belly button with one fingertip. I giggled at the ticklish sensation, trying to twist away as he pinched some of the flesh on my tummy.

"Have you gained a little weight recently?"

"Yeah, because *someone* made me go to that all-you-can-eat cake buffet with them," I retorted.

Wrapping his arms around me, he squeezed and pinched my stomach playfully. When I tried to resist his teasing, he laughed like a mischievous child, then finally let go.

"Seriously, girls have it so good," Riku sighed. "They're soft, and they smell nice."

"We're wearing the same scent, you know."

"That's not what I mean. Girls naturally smell pretty."

He buried his face in the curly waves he'd put in my hair earlier that afternoon, pursuing the fragrance I'd applied to the nape of my neck. He didn't usually buy lilac scents, but this one wasn't at all cloying, and he liked the unisex fragrance.

Hokkaido's lilac season peaked around mid-May, just before summer started. The last traces of the cold spring usually lingered a little while after the lilacs bloomed. It was well past that time of year, but today was surprisingly chilly, and I could feel the warmth of Riku's body behind me.

He was still stroking me up and down inside my clothes, but not lustfully. He just wanted to get his fill of the supple roundness unique to the female form. His favorite part was how my waistline curved between my flank and hip.

"Have your breasts gotten a little bigger, Ichika?"

"Probably because you keep poking and prodding them all the time."

"Shouldn't you be thanking me, in that case?"

I kept my eyes closed as much as I could when Riku touched me. That way, I could at least try and block out the image of the obviously male hand caressing my body. Since Riku and I were babies, we'd been raised practically like siblings. He *was* touching me, but only because he enjoyed dressing like a girl—because he enjoyed how soft and round female bodies felt.

At least, that's what I kept telling myself.

"I can't think of anything that makes me happier than touching you, Ichika." His lips brushed my earlobe with each word of his low whisper. He ran his fingertips tenderly over the lace of my camisole. "You're so beautiful."

I hadn't even realized my blouse was off. My camisole strap was around my shoulder, exposing my bare skin to the chilly air. Handling me like some fragile object, Riku lay me on the bed so gently that the creaky springs made only the slightest squeak. It felt like I was being assailed by a girl—here, in my room, our secret garden.

Riku only dabbled in cross-dressing in my room.

When we were little, he used to go out boldly wearing girls' clothing, but he'd stopped doing that in public as we approached puberty. Even his family didn't know about his hobby. We were next-door neighbors in the same apartment complex, and both our families assumed the reason he came to my room almost daily was because we were dating.

Most of the time, Riku was a perfectly nondescript teenager attending high school in Sapporo. He never used any vocabulary that would come off as feminine. He styled his short hair with wax and wore a disheveled school blazer. He used male pronouns. He was just your average seventeen-year-old boy.

Still, it wasn't uncommon to find him mingling with the girls at our school.

"What kind of tools do girls use to put on makeup?"

We were supposed to be discussing the upcoming school festival in sixth period homeroom. Our class, Class 2-A, had permission to serve refreshments at the booth we'd be running for the festival. As time ticked by, though, we still hadn't settled on a concept.

Hokkaido's rainy season had ended, and each day brought us closer to the preparation period that would run through the start of summer. The festival itself would take place on a three-day weekend in mid-July. Each class would run a booth, and the school's athletic and culture clubs were also working hard on performances and exhibits. Our homeroom teacher, who had a laissez-faire teaching style, had left us to our own devices; he appeared to be nodding off in one corner of the classroom.

Poplar fluff floated by outside the window. Our school was in the middle of Sapporo; from the school grounds, you could faintly make out the Sapporo TV Tower in Odori Park, and when the sky was clear, you could sometimes see Mt. Moiwa. It wasn't visible on hazy days like today, though.

Sakura Chiaki, our class representative, was supposed to be overseeing this discussion, but he had less influence than the popular kids. If someone voiced an opinion, they'd hit a dead end if that group didn't approve. The students at the top of the pecking order had grown bored with the discussion, though; the girls were arranging their cosmetics on their desks.

They'd already touched up their makeup at lunch, but now they seemed to be rushing to get ready for whatever lay ahead after school. Both girls and boys were supposed to wear a forest-green necktie with their school uniform, but some girls disregarded that requirement, using their own ribbon instead.

Iguchi Hikaru, an exceptionally gorgeous girl who happened to sit right behind Riku, was dabbing perfume on her wrists. Riku watched with fascination as she pulled one item after another from a makeup pouch that was almost bursting at the seams.

Iguchi-san was applying mascara when she adjusted her mirror and caught Riku spying on her. "Is my makeup routine really so interesting that you feel the need to stare?"

"Yup," he replied. "By the way, what do you tell your stylist to get them to dye your hair that color?"

Our school rules were pretty lax. As long as students passed hair and uniform inspections held at key stages of the school year, like right after summer vacation, they had a fair amount of freedom to style their hair and makeup as they pleased. The academic level at our school was relatively high within Sapporo, so no one risked pushing those freedoms to the limit. That meant everyone was able to enjoy dressing up within reasonable boundaries.

"Also, are those color contacts you're wearing?" Riku continued. "Isn't it a pain to put them in every day?"

"My hair and eye color are both natural. No one ever believes me when I tell them that, though."

Riku couldn't suppress his secret hobby completely; he took every opportunity he could to speak with the girls, and he got away with it thanks to his inherently affable personality. He seemed most interested in those who had the latest products from brands he'd read about in magazines, and those with eye-catchingly beautiful hair.

Having an audience while they applied makeup didn't bother the girls. They even shared tips as Riku reached over to look at some products. A few other boys eventually joined the conversation, and it went without saying that I was in the mix as well. Riku and I were in the same class, and he was by my side virtually all the time, fortunately for him. He knew that if he did something that might give him away somehow, I could help smooth things over.

"That blush shade just came out. It has pretty good pigmentation."

"A magazine just reviewed this mascara."

"This eyeliner doesn't make very clean lines. It's a shame since it was kind of expensive."

"Oh, yeah?" Riku said. Exchanges like these helped him build his knowledge base.

Other boys became curious and examined the assorted cosmetics themselves.

"Do you like girls who deck themselves out in lots of makeup, Tono-kun?" Iguchi-san probed. She stared him down with thickly lined eyes; her liner was drawn to perfection.

Riku looked completely unintimidated. "I'd say I prefer a more natural look," he grinned.

"Of course you do. Guys like you always end up going for girls who are cute without needing to do anything at all."

Riku was more than aware that a natural look was the hardest makeup to master, but he didn't let that show. He was also highly critical of the makeup style Iguchi-san was wearing, which emphasized the undereye—he said it looked like you'd "drawn eye circles on purpose." And he wasn't interested in Iguchi-san herself. It was her brand-new lip gloss that caught his attention.

Since the boys were also tired of the festival discussion—which was going nowhere—they started to play around, putting makeup on their own faces. One elicited a few laughs by painting his lips bright red. At that point, someone piped up with, "Hey, what if we held a dress-up café?"

At that suggestion, Riku's eyebrows twitched upward noticeably.

"The girls could dress us guys up in women's clothes, and we could serve customers!"

"Didn't some of our senpai do that a few years back? I heard it wasn't very popular. It weirded people out."

"Well, we can do it better! Just having a normal café would be boring, right?" countered another student.

The popular guys were getting on board with the idea. As students started exchanging a flurry of opinions, the class suddenly came alive. It was hard to believe that until only moments earlier, the discussion had been at a complete standstill. The wave of excitement even roused our teacher from his catnap.

"I'm not too sure about calling it a *dress-up* café, though," he commented, raising his head our direction.

"You're finally offering an opinion after snoozing this whole time, Rintaro?!"

Kakei Rintaro, our homeroom teacher, was still new to the job, and most students in our class didn't bother speaking to him with honorifics.

Still rubbing his sleepy eyes, he finally stepped up to the blackboard. "I have to submit the application for whatever you're doing by the end of the school day. Can you just decide already?"

"At this rate, it really will end up being a dress-up café," Chiaki sighed.

"What's wrong with that?" asked one student. It seemed like the class's mind was made up. "We *should* do something about that description, though. It's kind of lame."

"How about calling it a drag queen bar?'" suggested another. "We could dress up all flashy, like the entertainers you see on TV sometimes."

"I don't know if we should call it a 'bar.' It's not like we can serve alcohol."

"Okay, then... How about 'cross-dressing café'?"

"Perfect! 'Cross-dressing café' it is!"

With just a few minutes of homeroom left to spare, Class 2-A had finally picked a concept for its festival booth. The bell sounded just as we finished hurriedly putting everyone in groups to work on various café prep tasks.

As soon as school ended, the executive committee members headed to the festival representative meeting. Meanwhile, the students who'd been appointed group leaders had to attend an orientation session. As everyone bustled around, getting ready to leave for the day, I stole a glance in Riku's direction. His profile gave away none of his feelings on this turn of events. He stood and headed toward his assigned group without even realizing I was looking at him.

"Tono-kun seems like the type to be really picky about his girlfriend's look." Iguchi-san had finally finished her makeup. She watched Riku walk off, muttering under her breath, "I definitely couldn't deal with a guy like that."

Then she turned her gaze on me.

Riku was popular with the girls at school, but there was talk among some students that he and I were dating. That was probably why I was on the receiving end of Iguchi-san's stare.

Riku hadn't done anything to quell the rumors floating around about us. On the contrary, he might've realized he could benefit from them. Even if we'd denied that we were in a relationship, it's not like anyone would've believed us. After all, we arrived at school together in the morning and went straight to my room once we got home.

Still, seeing him reject every single girl who confessed her feelings made me wonder if he was even interested in the opposite sex. Though he touched my body, even at the susceptible age of seventeen, it didn't go further than that. He studied fashion magazines and online makeup tutorials passionately. He even wore skirts, beautifully transforming himself into a girl. Cross-dressing wasn't some fetish; taking on a feminine appearance seemed natural to him.

Yet I still didn't understand the depth of his fascination. I could see how it might've happened if he'd grown up surrounded by sisters, but Riku didn't have any.

Even when his fingers grazed my chest, he never did anything more. He'd slide his hand down my skirt and stroke my thighs, but that was the end of it. He touched me the way someone would cuddle and play with a doll. There was nothing sexual about his feelings toward me. Either I wasn't attractive to him as a woman, or he wasn't interested in girls in the first place. I had no doubt he'd reject me if he learned that we weren't on the same page—that *I* saw *him* as a man.

"Ichika, wait up!" Riku drawled behind me, his voice echoing through the school hallway. It reminded me of the way he spoke when he dressed up, so my gut reaction was to twist my head back in his direction.

I'd been assigned to the group in charge of the café menu, and when we drew lots to decide the group leader, I'd ended up with the short straw. My first task was to attend a workshop in the school kitchen right after school. When I left, Riku was busy chatting with some female students while they tidied the classroom, but he must've chased after me when he realized I was gone.

He was calling me in a low voice, and there was nothing graceful about his movements. I would've panicked if he'd been running girlishly, but everything about him looked masculine enough. His tone was perhaps slightly wheedling, but still at a level acceptable in the type of guy who tickled girls' maternal instincts.

"Why'd you leave without me?" he asked.

"It's not like we're even in the same group, Riku."

"No, but we'll probably be working together. It'd be good for me to listen in too."

Riku's group would work on the café interior—specifically, the decor. We'd need to ensure the decorations complemented the menu, so we probably *would* need to work closely for quite a bit of the prep period.

"It looked like you were having a real blast with Iguchi-san and her friends. Too bad you didn't end up in their group." I realized a few seconds too late how harsh those words sounded.

"Are you jealous, Ichika?" Riku responded with a little giggle.

"Absolutely not!"

Riku shrugged casually at my vehement denial. That shrug was undeniably sensual whenever he dressed as a girl, but under the current circumstances it just made him seem like an innocent little boy.

The workshop was being held in a kitchen in a separate building away from the classrooms. As we made our way over, the number of students around us dwindled. We were now right by the first-year students' fountains and bathrooms, and no one else appeared to be in the hallway.

Riku kept glancing around as if confirming that we truly were the only ones there. He twitched his finger as if checking something off an invisible list, then grabbed my arm and dragged me toward the fountains. I wondered if he was trying to pull me into one of the nearby bathrooms, but that didn't seem to be his plan—although he appeared to consider whether the boy's or girl's bathroom was a better hiding spot. He settled on pulling me next to the corner water fountain on the girls' side.

"Uh, Riku?"

The only response I got was, "Be quiet."

He snatched the notebook and pen I'd been holding and placed them on the windowsill under the blinds. The bewitching smile playing across his lips made it clear that I was in the presence of Riku's secret-garden personality.

"Did you see anything you liked today?" I sighed. In all honesty, it was less out of exasperation than relief that he'd chosen to be with me over the other girls.

"That brand-new gloss Iguchi had. It was just released yesterday!"

It was obvious from the excitement in his voice that he was going to buy himself one.

"Hey, Ichika, can I touch you?"

"Don't even think about it! What if someone comes by?"

He placed his hands against the wall on either side of me, preventing my escape. Then he stood directly in front of me, his tall frame completely blocking me from view.

"I got out of there because I thought the costume group was going to try taking my measurements," he explained.

The girls primping and preening earlier were in the group that would handle dressing the boys. Not only were they going to apply the guys' makeup, they also planned to put together their outfits from scratch. They hadn't decided who'd be cross-dressing yet, but Riku was likely at the top of their lists.

"You should do it, you know. Cross-dress for the festival."

"No way. It's not happening," Riku scowled as he attempted to unbutton my blouse. He was probably even better at undoing my tie than I was.

"Hey! I *said—*"

Before I finished speaking, a large hand covered my mouth and part of my nose. I squirmed in protest as his lips ran along my neck, but no lipstick left a trail on my exposed skin this time. Riku's short hair tickled as it brushed against me. This was nothing like the forbidden world we delved into while hidden away in my room. We were just like the couples who made out on the staircase landing by the school roof.

He usually whispered how cute or pretty I was, but this time, there was none of that. The silence around us was so heavy it was almost stifling.

Riku was about to slide his hand into my blouse when we heard excited chatter from the hallway. Two girls were approaching. Judging by their conversation, they seemed to be in a hurry—possibly rushing to the same kitchen workshop I was supposed to attend. I assumed they'd walk right by us, but the footsteps suddenly stopped.

We froze as one girl said, "Sorry. I need to use the bathroom. I'll be quick."

When the girl noticed us, she gasped. "Oh!" She turned back to her friend, whispering frantically, "Oh my gosh! We gotta go!"

They were probably first-years. As they ran off, I heard them squeal excitedly, chattering about what they'd just witnessed.

Riku obviously heard them too. Only when they were completely out of earshot did he finally mouth, "Are they gone?"

"Yeah, they're gone," I replied. Riku was still covering my mouth, muffling my voice. "I don't think they saw either of our faces."

"Good. Now let's get back to where we were," he said. His lips brushed against my hair.

I wasn't going down without putting up a proper fight. "Riku! Take your hand off my mouth!"

"You'll make a scene if I do that."

"I'll be late if I don't go now," I mumbled into his hand. He just grinned, continuing to ignore me. Even when I pushed against his chest, he wouldn't let go. He just pulled my hand away like it was no big deal, sending home that he really was a boy and much stronger than me. I could smell him—not the perfume we shared, but the smell of his sweat, the scent of a man. It made me lightheaded.

With no hesitation whatsoever, he showered me with little kisses the exact way a mother would kiss a baby, proving yet again that he wasn't at all *sexually* attracted to me.

"It's time to go, Riku."

"Fine. I guess this is enough for now."

He kissed the hand that was still placed right over my lips, but never kissed me directly on the mouth.

One time, Riku had experienced rejection because of his hobby. We'd been in our first year of junior high; the beginning of puberty had naturally put some distance between us, and we didn't talk as much. We still had a good time together when our families went out, but we basically avoided each other at school.

At that point, Riku was shorter than me, and had long hair for a boy. He was pale and slender, and his voice hadn't yet started to change. If he'd worn a skirt, he probably would've been mistaken for a girl.

The incident occurred while we were in a group with a girl who'd gone to a different elementary school than we had.

"Is it true you wore skirts in elementary, Riku-kun?" she asked almost menacingly.

It was true. Back then, Riku had worn girls' clothing like it was the most normal thing in the world. He came to class in pants, but always wanted to wear my skirts, so I often swapped bottoms with him after school.

"Yeah," Riku responded truthfully to the girl questioning him with the brusqueness of an interrogator. He looked a little confused, as if he was thinking, *Why would you even ask me that?*

The girl looked repulsed by his answer. Furrowing her brow and turning up her nose, she replied with a vehement "That's *gross*!"

She spoke so emphatically that droplets of spit flew from her mouth. All Riku could do was stare in stunned shock at her display of unfeigned disgust.

That single phrase triggered the whole class to gang up on him.

"Riku's got a bunch of dolls in his room. It looks like a girl's!"

"Riku's *always* played more with girls than boys!"

"I thought he just wore those skirts as a joke, but I guess not."

"The keychain on his bag is weird, and his pencil case is so babyish."

And even, "Don't talk to Riku, or you might turn gay!"

The mean comments rolled in one after another.

Fortunately, this teasing didn't last long. As puberty kicked in, Riku grew taller, and his voice deepened. He cut his hair, took the keychain off his bag, and made sure everything in his pencil case was nondescript, with no interesting colors or patterns.

Puberty helped, but Riku poured blood, sweat, and tears into changing himself. He gave me his beloved keychain, and somehow his strawberry-scented erasers ended up in my pencil case. The teddy bear he slept with every night found a new home in my room. He forced himself to walk and talk like the other boys. Eventually, his hard work paid off—he achieved the natural roughness typical of his peers.

We'd been distant for a while, but around that point, we started getting close again. He brought all his keepsakes over to my house, and it was surprising how cute and girly my room became, almost like he'd copied and pasted his room on top of mine.

That was why he came over every day. He knew I wouldn't say a word about him prancing around in skirts and the like, so he only ever wore them in front of me. At some point, he started dressing me as well. He learned to apply makeup and cultivated more and better techniques, pushing his femininity to new heights.

I had no issues with Riku's interest in cross-dressing. That incident in junior high had occurred at a time when the girls were just starting to get their periods, and they were extremely sensitive when it came to topics like boys or sex. By our third year of junior high, when my period finally came, our classmates were no longer scrutinizing Riku, and spending time with him felt as natural as breathing.

More than anything, I felt a sense of superiority about being someone special to him. I'd harbored feelings for Riku for a long time; as a little girl, my dream was to one day be his bride. As months and years passed, I simply came to accept the strange turn our relationship had taken.

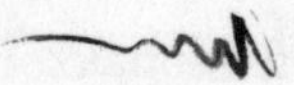

The winds of change blew through our secret garden once preparations for the school festival started. Riku and I used to head to my room as soon as school ended, but now there was meeting after meeting to discuss the café's menu, decor, and costumes. As the leader of the menu group, I was required to attend all of them.

Riku and the rest of the decor group mostly worked outside.

We often didn't see each other until the school grounds closed. Even then, I usually had to do things like grocery shop or go to another group member's house to test dishes we planned to serve, so we were like two ships passing in the night. Most days, Riku couldn't come to my room at all. In light of that, I was only spending time with the boy version.

One Sunday in July, not long before the school festival, a number of students met at the house of our class representative, Sakura Chiaki. In addition to all the group leaders, some others attended, including Riku. We all updated each other on the progress of our projects and were relieved to learn everything was going according to plan.

After the meeting ended that afternoon, Riku asked me to come along so we could shop together at a department store near Odori Park. In early summer, that park hosted the lilac festival and Yosakoi Soran dance festival. When those kinds of events weren't going on, it was just a place for people to come relax. The fountain's refreshing water jets sparkled in the sunlight. As children, Riku and I used to play in the fountain, but we'd aged out of that activity a long time ago.

Riku was hunting for the lip gloss he'd had his eye on since talking with Iguchi-san. We'd been so busy prepping for the school festival, we hadn't had time to look for it until now. We told the saleswoman at the cosmetics counter that I was looking for lip gloss, and she brought me several products to try.

Riku had something to say about each one.

"You might need a brighter color."

"That looks good on you."

"Why not try that shade too?"

The saleswoman showered him with praise like "You must really love your girlfriend!" It was obvious that I wasn't very experienced with makeup, so she showed me some beginner tips while, from the sidelines, Riku took mental notes on her professional techniques. With a few final words of encouragement—"Your boyfriend will be happy if you keep practicing your makeup!"—she sent me off with a few free samples, which I promptly handed over to Riku.

For the first time in a while, we headed to my room. I barely had time to toss my backpack on my bed and get changed before Riku started on my makeup.

"I knew this was the right color for you," he said, arranging his cosmetics and mirror on the folding table. I couldn't even count the products in his collection; he probably had close to as many as a professional makeup artist. He started working on my face in a quick but careful manner, utilizing techniques he'd gleaned by watching the saleswoman.

"I wanted to get a different shade from Iguchi-san's, to be honest. This one produces the best color, though. It could go with that tight skirt we bought a while back. As for your hair, I'll try for a glossy look that's not too curled."

Although this was my room, Riku knew far more than I did about what was in the closet. He even picked out my underwear.

"You don't want any panty lines showing through the skirt." He probably kept track of the smallest fluctuations in my size.

As he pulled out the clothes he wanted me to try, I asked hesitantly, "Is that all you're going to do?"

"Don't worry. I'll finish your makeup later."

"That's not what I meant. What about you?"

My question finally reminded Riku that he was still dressed like a boy. He gave a slight gasp, grabbing a dress from my closest as I changed into my outfit.

Riku might've been an expert on my undergarments, but he didn't wear bras himself, and it was always boxer briefs under his skirts. When he yanked off his T-shirt, he exposed a set of well-defined pectorals rather than breasts.

Riku got himself ready in much less time than it took to dress me up. He was just wearing his long black wig and light makeup—specifically, foundation and eye shadow. Still, it only took lipstick to transform the boy sitting before me into a woman who exuded a hint of sensuality.

He was just wearing a dress. It was one of his favorites, made from soft fabric with a wide hem. He'd paired it with bold-colored stockings that emphasized his long, shapely legs. Riku removed his hair religiously, so his arms and legs were perennially smooth.

"Yup. It doesn't feel right unless I look fabulous too!" he said with a flirtatious giggle.

Nothing could stop Riku once he was like this. With even more gusto than usual, he used a curling iron to twist my hair into soft ringlets, then applied oil to give them a glossy sheen. Although he'd finished up my makeup, he didn't seem satisfied, and kept waffling over which earrings I should wear. It was obvious how much he'd looked forward to spending time with me in our secret garden again.

Smiling, Riku showed me my face in the mirror. "That should do it. Look how beautiful you are now." His gaze seemed intense, maybe because he was wearing less makeup than usual.

"You've outdone yourself again today, Riku."

"Thanks."

I did my own makeup from time to time, but I could never get my eyes to look as big as he could. It surprised me how different I looked just from Riku straightening out some of the natural waves in my hair. He usually stuck with cute styling that suited a high school girl, but he'd gone for a more adult look today to complement the new lip gloss shade.

Even I had to admit I looked prettier than usual. Since Riku had been doing my makeup for so long, he had a good sense of which features to accentuate and which to cover up. He never copied the magazine-feature styles that emulated famous actresses' makeup. Even when he followed the latest trends, he always adapted them to me.

He really is amazing, I thought as I gazed at my face in the mirror. As he watched me admire myself, Riku scooted closer, a twinkle in his eye. *Here it comes,* I thought. *The usual line.*

"Ichika, can I touch you?"

I paused. "Sure." Curled strands of hair stuck to my glossy lips as I spoke. I was wearing more mascara than usual; when I blinked, it felt heavy.

Riku had me sit on the bed as he knelt in front of me and placed his hands on my thighs. He smiled silently as he stroked my stockinged knees, tracing a line all the way to my toes, then kissing them. It felt like a beautiful lady was waiting on me. When I quietly attempted to adjust my hair, he looked up at me, eyes smoldering. Even his gaze through the gap in his bangs was sexy.

Tucking his hair behind his ears, he gave my knees a last kiss before abruptly standing up. He pushed me down on the bed and climbed on top of me, the backlight obscuring his expression. We wore the same fragrance, but it smelled different on him. The ends of his wig fluttered across my chest.

"Ichika," he whispered, stroking my cheek. His fingertips trembled slightly, probably with excitement at touching me like this for the first time in quite a while.

He leaned forward on his elbows and brought his face close to mine. I felt his weight, but he wasn't crushing me. He was consciously ensuring he wasn't doing anything that hurt—a kindness that put me a little more at ease.

Now that we were close enough to feel the warmth of each other's breath, I could finally make out Riku's expression. In the silence, I gazed into his eyes and saw myself reflected—yet the girl looking back didn't resemble me at all. *Who is it that he's always seeing?* I wondered in the small corner of my mind still capable of rational thought.

He was looking at me, the secret-garden doll he could dress however he pleased.

What does Riku want from me? Who is he dressing up in all these clothes? What words does he want to hear from these painted lips? What can I do to make him notice me?

"Riku?"

He smiled as I murmured his name, and I instinctively squeezed my eyes shut as his fingers slid under my blouse. Before I knew it, he undid all my buttons, covering my exposed chest with lipstick marks from his kisses. His lipstick was a deep wine color, one of his favorites.

He never used that shade on me, however. The colors that suited him weren't right on me. He was seeking the image of his ideal woman. Someone who'd look good in his favorite colors and pull off the clothing he liked perfectly—his goddess.

I couldn't live up to those expectations.

"You're beautiful, Ichika," he whispered as he nibbled my earlobe. The ticklish sensation sent shivers running down my spine.

Riku might've been dressed like a girl, but the hands caressing my body were big and strong. The person looking down at me appeared female, undoubtedly, but I knew that the dress concealed a rugged, lean body underneath.

"Ichika..." he whispered in a raspy voice both sweet and deep. Although he wore eye shadow, his gaze was still sharp.

"Riku..."

I pushed against his chest, but he grabbed both my hands and easily pinned them to the bed. He held them in place with one hand, stroking my skin with the other. When I tried to move away, he rested some of his weight on me, making escape impossible.

His lips grazed my chest. They left a trail of warm breath in their wake, making my entire body feel like it would spontaneously combust.

We'd been apart for too long. Instead of hanging out in my room, we'd just interacted at school. That short span of time was all it had taken me to adjust to seeing Riku solely as a boy.

So, who is *this person on top of me?*

"Riku, wait!" I exclaimed. My words didn't reach him—they never did. I was just a doll he could play with. He was projecting the image of his perfect goddess onto me.

"Let go of me, Riku!" I struggled with all my might, but he didn't flinch. He kissed my cheek, the corner of my eye, and my forehead in turn before returning his lips to my cheek once more.

But he wasn't kissing me—he was kissing his ideal, the girl of his dreams. He didn't see the real me, the girl desperately suppressing her yearning for him, which grew each time he touched her.

"Riku!"

The word was muffled by a pair of wine-colored lips. That was our first kiss on the lips—the one place he'd always left untouched.

I jerked my head to the side. "Stop it!" I screamed.

My outburst must've startled him. He loosened his grip, and I was able to wriggle free from his grasp and roll off the bed.

He gaped as he surveyed the distance I'd suddenly put between us. "Ichika, what—"

"Don't touch me!"

He reached out for me, but I dodged his arms, rising to my feet. I heard him call after me, but I fled our secret garden without giving him a second glance.

I sprinted frantically, sweating buckets in the lingering heat of the afternoon sun. My tight skirt clung to my skin, making it hard to run, and it was tough to breathe properly with my hair constantly falling in my face. By the time I got breathless and slowed down, I'd reached the park where I'd often played as a child.

Lilac season was over, but I could still make out a few late-blooming plants. They gave off a natural sweetness different from our perfume. Each time I breathed the scent in, it took me back to my childhood.

The park flowers bloomed year-round. In spring, there was a carpet of dandelions. I used to search for four-leaf clovers while a crown of white flowers adorned my head. In summer, false acacia petals poured down like rain, and delicate lavender blossoms filled the flowerbeds. In fall, we snacked on ripe raspberries and yew berries.

In those days, our garden wasn't a secret.

The jungle gym with a long slide was still there after all these years. Back in the day, Riku and I used to play there until the sun went down. I recalled a time I'd walked home hand in hand with Riku after he fell and skinned his knee, the setting sun casting long, willowy shadows behind us.

I'd tried to comfort him. "Don't cry, Riku. Once we get home, I'll bandage it up for you."

"But my clothes are all muddy!"

The reason he'd fallen in the first place was that some older boys ganged up on him while we played tag.

"Why'd they tease me for wearing pink? I don't get it. No one gives you a hard time about it, Ichika," he moaned.

"Probably because you're a boy."

"Why's that matter? Why can't boys wear pink? Why can't I wear skirts to preschool? Why can't I be like you?"

I remembered feeling like his big sister as we walked home holding hands, the chime that signaled five o'clock ringing out around us. I ran through the park, trying to shake that melody from my mind.

I can't go back. No—I don't want to go back.

The days of walking home together as the sun set were long gone.

I still felt Riku on my lips; that kiss had unlocked the door of my heart. Now, I wanted him to touch me, hold me, know who I truly was.

Lilacs were said to be the flower of love. Their scent had surrounded me as, many years ago, I fell in love while playing in this park. I loved Riku so much—so much that it hurt.

"Ow!" someone yelped.

I wasn't paying attention to my surroundings as I ran, so I hadn't noticed someone else walking by.

"I'm so sorry!" I exclaimed.

The force of our collision had made the girl drop her bag. As I bent to pick it up for her, our eyes met.

"Iguchi-san?"

Iguchi-san was in charge of clothing and makeup for our class café, so she'd also attended the meeting at the class representative's house earlier today. *I don't remember her living nearby. I wonder what she's doing here.*

Iguchi-san also looked surprised. She rubbed the shoulder I'd run into as her pretty eyes gave me a once-over. "Why're you so dressed up, Hasumi-san?"

Her question brought me crashing back to reality. I didn't wear makeup to school, nor did I bother to straighten my hair, so she'd never had an opportunity to see me this dolled up.

"You look really different with makeup," she remarked as she scrutinized my face. "It's nice. Why not go to school like that?" Then, in the blink of an eye, her gaze moved behind me.

"Ichika!" Riku bellowed as he dashed straight in my direction. He was winded from running, so he couldn't use his customary feminine tone. When I glanced over my shoulder, I saw he was still wearing the dress from earlier.

As I realized that Riku hadn't yet noticed Iguchi-san, my blood ran cold. *Oh, no. This is really bad,* I thought. Before I could do anything, she'd already caught sight of him.

Riku stopped running, catching his breath with his hands on his knees. His disheveled wig concealed his face, but Iguchi-san's gaze trailed to his feet. Riku didn't have any women's shoes, since he dressed up exclusively in the secret garden of my room. His only option for going outside was men's sneakers. Noticing the dissonance between his shoes and outfit, Iguchi-san put two and two together just as Riku looked up.

"Tono-kun?" she inquired, although she already knew it was him. "What are you wearing?" Riku's face went pale as a sheet. There was nothing I could do or say as Iguchi-san strutted over to get a better look. "Why're you dressed like a girl?"

Riku's mouth gaped open and closed like that of a goldfish out of water. I could tell the beads of water trickling down his skin weren't from running; he'd broken into a cold sweat.

I had to do something to protect him.

"We were practicing!" I exclaimed. They both turned to look at me. "You know, for the school festival. I tried making Riku up, but it didn't go very well, as you can see."

Once the words began to pour out, I couldn't stop them. I continued my explanation, trying to sound as casual as possible.

"Instead of just going all-in on the day of, I thought it might be a good call to see how he'll look ahead of time. He was worried about what to wear, so I let him try some of my clothes on too."

It was almost painful, but I stared straight into Iguchi-san's eyes, forcing myself not to let a single shred of anxiety show. "I know you're in charge of the costumes. Sorry about stepping on your toes. I'm happy to help if you need anything on the day of, though."

"That's...fine," she replied a little hesitantly.

My plan had succeeded. Iguchi-san's tense expression relaxed as she looked back and forth between Riku and me.

"I guess it's impossible for boys to look good in the same makeup styles as girls," she murmured. She tapped her mouth thoughtfully with a finger, looking Riku up and down. "I thought just a little makeup would be fine in Tono-kun's case, at least. But seeing him now..." she trailed off.

As she continued her relentless appraisal, Riku appeared to smile, but I could tell it was just his lips reflexively twitching.

"I guess our usual clothes and makeup won't be enough. You may have feminine features, Tono-kun, but you don't look *girlish* right now. Women's clothes don't flatter male bodies. The more feminine men try to look, the less natural it seems. That's probably why our senpai's cross-dressing café flopped," Iguchi-san muttered, nodding to herself. "Thanks, Hasumi-san. This has been a big help. I'll make time for us to practice before the festival starts."

"Good idea," I replied. "Let me know if there's anything I can do to help."

"You two should probably head back home. Tono-kun looks like he's being punished for losing a bet or something."

Iguchi-san gave us a casual wave goodbye and walked away, leaving Riku and me standing there in stunned silence.

The day grew dark as the sun slowly sank in the sky, but we stayed at the park.

"Are you okay, Riku?" I asked, peeking behind the large slide.

Riku sat in one cranny of the jungle gym, face buried in his knees. No children were around now. The playful scent of greenery wafted through the air whenever the breeze rustled the trees in the deserted park.

"Riku," I tried again, but he didn't respond. I wondered what was going through his head as he sat there, hiding his face.

Once Iguchi-san disappeared from view, Riku had slunk behind the slide without saying a word. He'd done the same thing as a child whenever something bad happened. The other boys had often teased Riku because he was small, and he'd run away to conceal himself behind this slide until everyone was gone.

It had always been me who came to get him.

"Riku, let's go home." I'd reach out to him, and he'd finally stop cowering and take my outstretched hand. We'd walk home hand in hand just as the five o'clock chime began. But that didn't happen today. However many times I called out to him, he wouldn't move a muscle.

I was supposed to be running away *from him.* The irony didn't escape me, but I pushed my feelings aside and bent down to squeeze behind the slide as well. The space, which had been wide enough to comfortably fit us both as children, now felt incredibly tight. We were practically poking our knees into each other, sending home the fact that we were well past the appropriate age to be in here. I'd thought the secret garden only existed in my room, but I realized Riku saw this as a special place for the two of us from way back.

The wind didn't reach behind the slide, so the air was thick with the scent of the park—greenery mixed with a trace of lilacs. The scent of our perfume overlapped with the fragrance of our childhood.

"Let's go home, Riku. It's getting dark." I placed a hand on his shoulder, but all he did in response was shake his head silently.

"Is what Iguchi-san said bothering you? Don't worry about it, okay? We were rushing today. You only had light makeup on. On top of that, you were wearing sneakers."

His wig was disheveled and tangled. Riku's sweat had probably washed off all his perfume; his scent filled my nostrils.

"Everything's going to be okay," I said encouragingly.

Riku remained silent before finally replying in a trembling whisper, "No, it's not."

"Don't worry about Iguchi-san. She's not going to tell anyone what she saw. You can pull out all the stops for the festival and make everyone ooh and aah over you!"

"No."

"Let's go, Riku. You'll hurt yourself, staying cramped in this tight space."

The park darkened rapidly as the sun continued its descent. It was summer, but it still got chilly at night; if we stayed out too long in these light clothes, we might catch cold.

"Come on, let's go." I peered into his face, finally getting a brief look at his expression.

"I can't do it anymore," Riku mumbled. I thought he was crying, but his eyes showed no sign of tears. "I can't be you."

"Riku?" I asked uncertainly, reaching out to turn his face toward me.

He resisted at first, but as I pulled him closer, he seemed to give up and simply averted his eyes. "I can't be you, Ichika."

"Can't be me?"

Riku shook his head and bit his lip, which still had the faintest trace of lipstick. "I've always wanted to be you, Ichika. I wanted to wear the same clothes as you, Ichika. I wanted your face, Ichika." He was repeating my name so much, it almost sounded like incoherent mumbling. "We were the same when we were kids. I could wear the same clothes you could. No one got upset if I had long hair. I was able to be a girl, just like you, Ichika."

We'd been just like sisters back then. I was taller, so he happily wore the hand-me-downs I gave him. When we played together while he was in a skirt, people took both of us for girls, but that didn't bother either of us; we were just happy to be special to each other. But our bodies and hearts began to change as years and months passed by.

"I gradually stopped being able to wear your clothes. I bought some bigger ones, but they didn't look right on me. Even if we wear the same makeup, I don't look the same as you, Ichika."

I paused. "Do you want to be a girl, Riku?" It was something I'd always wondered, but never dared ask.

Riku shook his head. "I wanted to be you, Ichika. You're my perfect girl." He finally met my eyes. "You're the girl I've been around as long as I can remember. I thought we could always stay the same. But I just can't do it."

"You wanted...to be me?"

Riku looked away again and silently nodded. "But you're you, so I *can't* be you. Your body kept becoming a girl's—but mine didn't. It's like the differences drove a wedge between us."

So, he'd started to feel a sense of discomfort with his beloved doll.

"I looked for myself in you, but I couldn't find a single similarity," Riku continued. "Nothing about us was the same. You got prettier as each day passed, but I just started looking worse in makeup and girl's clothes. It made me frustrated, jealous—and, most of all, sad that I wasn't part of you."

He'd been looking for himself in me.

"Ichika...I love you." The words sounded painfully forced. "I was relieved to think some parts of us might be the same. That you saw me for who I was. But the more your body changed, the more it felt like the differences were pushing us apart. When I looked for myself in you, I found myself wanting to hold you, do unspeakable things to you, make you mine."

He must've thought I'd put even more distance between us if I knew he felt that way.

His eyes were squeezed shut, but by the time he finished speaking, they'd opened, and large tears streamed down his cheeks.

"I'm sorry, Ichika. I'm so sorry."

"Riku..."

Now that he could no longer hold back his tears, Riku sobbed like a child. "I'm so sorry, Ichika. I hurt you, didn't I?"

Each time he wiped his eyes, streaks of eye shadow rubbed off, and his foundation was completely gone. Seeing him barefaced, I reached out to him.

"I want to hold you too." I took his tear-drenched hand. "Touch me, Riku."

He hesitated, trying to pull away as I pressed his hand against my chest.

"You don't need to apologize. Search even harder; you're in here somewhere." I tucked his messy hair behind his ear and looked deep into his eyes. "I love you, Riku. I know you're inside of me."

Our affection for each other had gradually changed. We'd grown up best friends—sisters—and I was sure I'd betrayed those feelings first, since I fell in love with him. The way I saw him had changed. I'd wanted to hold him, have him all to myself, but I didn't want him to know. So I'd tried to erase the parts of him inside me.

I was me, and Riku was Riku. We couldn't stay the same forever, and we couldn't adjust ourselves to match each other. The more our bodies developed, the more different they became. But I knew the feelings I had for him would never change.

Riku cupped my breasts shyly, his usual boldness completely gone. That made me giggle; there was something heartwarming about it.

He had an innocent heart. There was something almost fragile about it—like you could break it with a single touch. You wanted to keep it to yourself and destroy it with your own two hands, all at the same time.

I finally understood how he felt when he touched me. In his heart, Riku had been protecting me like his greatest treasure.

I cupped his cheeks in both hands. We were so close we could feel each other's breath. His lips began to shape my name once more, but I silenced him with a kiss.

Night fell on the park before we knew it. We held hands and walked along the road, which was lit only by faintly glowing streetlights. The scent of the familiar flowers, the road we'd walked down many times before—something about today made them feel brand new.

We returned to the apartment complex where we both lived, but not to the secret garden.

How many years has it been since I was last in Riku's room?

It was the quintessential high-school boy's room. Everything in it was basic, from the desk to the bed to the curtains. It was a little messy—there were disorganized piles of Riku's things on the floor, and the manga in the bookcase was haphazardly arranged.

There was no trace of sweet perfume here; the room just smelled like Riku's natural scent.

We didn't say a single word until the door shut behind us; we remained quiet even after Riku locked it. As we stood in the still silence permeating his room, it felt like all it would take was to speak one word, and this world would crash down around us.

We exchanged kisses so naturally, it didn't seem as though our first kiss had been earlier that day. It was like we already knew how each other's lips would feel, and we were just confirming that knowledge. It seemed almost incomprehensible that we'd never tried it until now.

The room was dark, but the moonbeams flooding through the window illuminated us in silvery light. Riku touched me with the care of someone handling delicate sugar candy. Though he said nothing, his eyes, now completely devoid of eye shadow, spoke volumes. He was being incredibly considerate, but his gaze concealed a sharp glint.

I reached out for him, my fingers tangling in his hair. His wig was slipping, and he tossed it on his bed without a hint of concern, revealing his true face. There was no trace of the feminine Riku to be seen.

Why were we born into different bodies?

Riku caressed me again, his touch exploring each curve of my form. Our bodies had been the same when we were children, but his touch spoke to the fact that our chests, waists, and butts were completely different now.

Still, the feeling in both our hearts was the same.

Riku's body was different from mine. Even when I grabbed his toned underarm, he didn't flinch. The strength of his embrace took my breath away, but he was always gentle enough to loosen his grip immediately.

"Ichika." His whisper seemed to penetrate me. "You're beautiful."

You're beautiful too, Riku.

Before I could put my thought into words, he kissed me again.

We were searching for each other, doing whatever we could to find the truth that lay within us both, trying to become one.

Why were we born into different bodies? To seek something out that we both shared? Something eyes couldn't see, that only existed deep within our hearts?

We pursued the answers to those questions as we explored the comfort of each other's warmth for the first time.

PART 2

Sakura, Sakura

Riku Can't Be a Goddess

OUR CHERRY BLOSSOMS BLOOMED on a day when the last remnants of winter snow fell.

"There it is!" I gasped in astonishment, clutching my entrance examination slip in one mitten.

Large snowflakes floated down from the clouds hanging over the students milling around the campus bulletin board. The school grounds were full of prospective students who'd taken the school's entrance exam. Each one scanned the posted list for their examinee number and, if they found it, yelped in delight. Depending on their results, their faces reflected delight or despair.

"My number's there!"

That one especially loud scream made my heart tremble. Someone with the same mittens as mine flailed her hands up and down in an exuberant celebration, not caring one bit for the stares of others.

"I did it! I passed! I got in, Hazuki!"

"Me too, Yoshino!"

Yoshino threw her arms around me in a big hug, jumping up and down in her sheepskin boots. My head bobbed with her movements, causing snow to land and melt on my eyelids. Yoshino took off her mittens to wipe what looked to be tears of joy from her eyes. Her fingers were covered with some of the biggest calluses I'd ever seen.

"All the studying was worth it!" she exclaimed. "I'm so excited that I can go to the same school as you!"

When Yoshino first chose the high school she wanted to attend, her homeroom teacher told her not to overexert herself, suggesting she aim for a lower-ranked school. We'd made a pact to attend the same high school, though, so she devoted Christmas and New Year's to studying. That ultimately paid off, and she passed the entrance exam at her first-choice school.

"Now we can be together all the time, right, Hazuki?"

Neatly trimmed chin-length hair accentuated her small face. I nodded, feeling as though I was being drawn into her large, loquat leaf-shaped eyes.

"Of course! Even in high school!"

My hair—which was cut the same length as hers—was hidden inside my hood, but Yoshino and I wore the same earmuffs. Our mittens, cream-colored scarves, caramel-colored duffle coats, and sheepskin boots were identical as well.

Everything around us began to turn white as the snow fell even harder. It had been melting steadily until just recently, but the world was now once again transforming into a winter wonderland.

"Those are cherry trees," Yoshino murmured excitedly. She gazed at the trees surrounding the school grounds, which were quickly becoming dusted with snow. "They won't flower in time for the entrance ceremony, but it'll be great to see them in full bloom when we come to class."

The tightly sealed buds probably wouldn't blossom until late April. I could already picture the two of us going to school. We'd walk together, wearing the same uniform, with the same keychain dangling from our bags. We wore our hair in the same style, and our skirts at exactly the same length. We were around the same height and had similar figures, so we looked just like twins.

Yoshino and I had two hearts that beat as one. We were two beings bound together by a common destiny.

I first met Yoshino during the summer of the second year of junior high, well past the period when cherry blossoms bloomed.

"I'm Somei Yoshino. Nice to meet you," she introduced herself, standing in front of the blackboard. At the sound of her unusual name—identical to a type of cherry tree—laughter broke out and rippled through the classroom, making her blush and drop her gaze to the floor.

Since her new uniform hadn't arrived yet, she still wore one from her previous school. The sailor-style uniform was completely different from ours, which made her stick out like a sore thumb. To top it off, she'd transferred in the middle of the school year, so everyone in our class stared like she was a fish out of water.

"Well, who'd like to show her around the school?"

Our homeroom teacher glanced across the classroom before making eye contact with me. Her painted lips curled into a smile. "How about you, Hazuki?"

That was how Yoshino and I became each other's one and only best friend.

We started high school, and even had the good fortune to be placed in the same first-year class. We were still getting into the rhythm of this new life stage, one completely different from junior high, as preparations for the school festival began. Our class, 1-C, would be running a haunted house.

"Hey!" a boy called out to us. "Can I get a little help over here?"

Yoshino and I looked up in unison. "Which one of us are you asking?" I called back.

"It doesn't matter. I just need someone to hold this post down so I can attach it to the sign."

Our group, which was working on the haunted house's set pieces and scenery, was the biggest. The rule was that any work with tools had to take place outside, so students from every grade were congregating in the courtyard. The scenery group's leader was a boy on the baseball team, and his voice carried well through the courtyard.

I stood first and headed toward the group leader, who was in the middle of completing the sign. As I hopped around the tools scattered over the ground, my skirt hem flipped up accidentally; the group leader hastily averted his eyes when he noticed.

A few classes hadn't yet begun their prep work, but us first years had started quite early on. I pressed the post against the sign that would advertise our class's haunted house as the group leader began to hammer it into place.

"You're really good at this, huh?" I remarked.

"My dad works in construction, so I've been messing around with stuff like hammers and saws since I was a little kid."

Our group leader seemed right at home sawing pieces of wood. Hammering away with no trace of hesitation, a couple spare nails sticking out of his mouth, he had the look of a seasoned professional. Under his direction, the scenery group was making excellent progress on the haunted house's signs and the maze walls.

"We've got most of the physical pieces done, but I still have some doubts about whether we can pull all the tricks off. Since we're working with a limited budget, I know we have to cut corners, but I don't want it to turn out shoddy."

As we spoke, the groups in charge of playing ghosts and working on the costumes were meeting in the classroom. They planned to use old standbys like creating a spooky atmosphere by hanging small, dim lights, and dangling clammy chunks of konjac jelly from the ceiling. Still, most school festival haunted houses couldn't escape a cobbled-together atmosphere. The fact that the ghosts weren't allowed to directly touch any guests would make eliciting scares even harder.

"We've worked so hard on these set pieces, I'd like to incorporate some kind of gimmick," he continued. "Maybe a hole ghosts could pop out of. Something like that."

"You should go with whatever you think works," I replied. "Just leave the painting to us, okay?"

Yoshino and I were in charge of painting the set pieces. Yoshino sat silently using a brush in a corner of the schoolyard, far away from the boys working on actual construction tasks.

The group leader glanced in her direction. "Somei seems really good with her hands. She probably would've been better off working on costumes," he murmured under his breath.

The reason Yoshino and I had picked the scenery group in the first place was because it was the biggest. We had worried that if we chose something popular, like playing ghosts or making costumes, choosing group members might come down to a lottery and we could be split up. Scenery was the group with the most openings, so that's what we went with. Yoshino wasn't very strong, though, so tasks like hammering and carrying pieces of wood were tough for her. Sometimes the boys asked me to help with the construction work, but Yoshino was hardly ever tasked with anything involving physical labor.

The way she crouched against the wall of the outdoor walkway reminded me of a tiny hamster hiding in its cage. The wind was strong that day. It whipped against the plastic sheets we'd spread on the ground, flipping them several times. One strong gust sent a garbage bag full of tools flying; it landed right by Yoshino's side.

"Sorry, Somei. Could you grab that for us?" one boy asked.

Yoshino said nothing at first, then returned the bag to the boy with a barely audible whisper. Even when he thanked her, all she could muster in return was a small nod. She was a square peg in a round hole in this group consisting mainly of male students.

Because she was terrified of men, Yoshino could barely communicate with our male groupmates. All the boys in our class knew that, and no one bothered her about it—evidence of high schoolers' maturity approaching that of adults.

"The sign's ready, Yoshino," I said, carrying over the freshly constructed sign so we could start painting it. "They told us to make it look really cool."

Our group leader was very particular about his creations, and he wanted us to cover the sign with a base coat before working on any details. We were in the middle of covering our rollers with the base coat when a voice called down on us from above.

"You'll get your uniforms dirty if you paint like that."

When we glanced up, a boy was peeking from under the railing of the walkway connecting the school buildings. His backpack was slung over his shoulder, so he was probably on his way home. He likely wasn't a fellow first year, since I didn't recognize him.

"You should probably get changed," he continued. "Do you have your gym sweats?"

"Um, we didn't have P.E. today," I replied.

I'd interacted with students from other classes before; after all, we were all working in the courtyard. Still, having someone I didn't know speak directly to me was nerve-racking.

"How about I lend you mine?" the boy suggested. "I had P.E. today, but I only wore a T-shirt. My sweatshirt should still be clean."

"B-but..." I immediately tried to protest.

"If you were a boy, it wouldn't matter, but I'd feel bad if a girl got paint all over her uniform," he insisted.

He pulled his sweatshirt out of his backpack and handed it to Yoshino. It was light blue, confirming my suspicion that he was a second-year. Then, completely disregarding our obvious nervousness about the situation, he chased after the boy walking ahead of him and grabbed his sweatshirt too.

"Here's another one. It's so big that it might be awkward to move in, but at least it won't matter if you get it dirty."

"Thanks."

"Also, make sure you wear work gloves. It's hard washing off paint. You don't want to have to use harsh astringent to remove it and damage your skin."

With a quick goodbye, he chased after the boy whose sweatshirt he'd borrowed. From the snippets of casual conversation I picked up, I guessed they were probably classmates.

"If our class doesn't start working soon, we'll be in a world of trouble," one said.

"We need to decide what we're doing next time we have homeroom. Make sure you weigh in too, Riku," replied the other.

"Whatever it is, I think I want to be in the group that makes the scenery. Working outside looks relaxing and fun."

I figured they must be students from 2-A, the only class not yet represented in the school courtyard.

Yoshino and I exchanged surprised glances at that turn of events. Yoshino quickly unfolded the sweatshirt she'd received, glancing at the kanji embroidered on the fabric.

"This one belongs to…Tono-senpai," she said, then hesitantly pulled it over her head. "Are you sure this is okay?"

"It's fine," I reassured her. "They lent them to us, so it'd be rude not to wear them."

Yoshino froze up whenever she talked to boys, but she didn't seem to balk at wearing their clothes.

I unfolded the other sweatshirt, then gasped at the name the fabric revealed. "Hey! This is Chiaki's!"

"Chiaki…? You mean your big brother?"

My brother was a year older than me, and we attended the same high school. As I peered again at the boys from earlier, Chiaki turned around and waved at me. Well, that solved the mystery of why the boy had been so friendly with us. I was sure Chiaki was behind it; I even understood exactly how it must've played out. He'd seen his little sister working and mentioned it to his classmate, who probably thought messing with us would be funny.

"I've always wanted a sibling. I'm so jealous," Yoshino murmured.

"Don't be. All we do is fight, usually. He's just trying to look good at school." He and I were only a year apart, so we acted more like twins than regular siblings.

I slid on the sweatshirt, which had the same fabric-softener scent of my own clothes. The sweatshirts were so big on Yoshino and me that their sleeves kept slipping down whenever we tried to paint with the rollers.

Each time they did, Yoshino re-cuffed her sleeves diligently. "We can't let these get stained," she insisted.

"Want me to take them both home and give them to Chiaki? It'd be awkward to return them to a second-year classroom ourselves, right?"

The first- and second-year classrooms were on the same floor, but the upper and lowerclassmen had a rigidly defined sense of territory. We weren't at liberty to use the same staircase they did, and there was even an unwritten rule that the bathroom on our floor was for second-years only. If first-years needed to use the restroom, we had to use a different one.

"That's probably a good idea. It's not like I'd even be able to thank him." Yoshino smiled weakly. She knew better than anyone how intense her phobia was. She couldn't even talk to our male homeroom teacher properly, let alone male students in our class. She could tolerate being around guys she was used to, but she'd never initiate conversation with them.

She sighed, running her slender, pale fingers over the embroidered chest of her borrowed sweatshirt. "If only I'd grown up with a brother."

In addition to the haunted house scenery, our group was responsible for decorating the classroom interior.

"Crap! If we don't hurry, we won't make it before the workshop starts!" I yelped as we ran through the hallway. Our main task was working on set pieces in the courtyard, but now we were en route to a meeting in the school kitchen.

"Why'd the storage room have to be locked today, of all days?!" I moaned.

A thick blackout curtain was a must-have for a successful haunted house. We'd stopped by the school storage room to borrow one, but discovered the door was locked. The home economics teacher had the key, but when we went to the staff room to ask for it, they told us she'd left to give a workshop on food safety. That sent us into a panic, and we raced off in the direction of the school kitchen to try and catch her.

"How come we have to ask a teacher for the key anytime we want to get in there?!"

"They keep valuables in there," was Yoshino's levelheaded response. "It'd be bad if those got stolen, right?"

Still, if we didn't get that key before the workshop started, it would delay everything we planned to do that afternoon. The school kitchen was in a building far from our homeroom, so we wouldn't make it unless we sprinted there.

As we passed the first-year drinking fountains, I couldn't ignore the little voice in my bladder any longer. "Sorry. I need to use the bathroom. I'll be quick."

I thought Yoshino would keep going, but she turned and followed me instead.

"Oh!" I gasped, pausing as I noticed someone in the blind spot near the fountains. A boy stood alongside the fountain closest to the girl's bathroom. I could tell from his light-blue indoor shoes that he was a second-year, but he was turned toward the wall, his arms pressed against it, so I couldn't see his face. Just beyond his tall frame, I caught sight of what appeared to be part of a girl's uniform—between his legs, I could spot someone's knee, but that was it.

One look at the pale thigh peeking out below the disheveled skirt told Yoshino and I everything we needed to know. We immediately turned on our heels and dashed toward the kitchen, trying to calm down by exchanging wide-eyed glances and squealing about the shocking scene we'd stumbled upon.

We somehow made it to the kitchen to borrow the key just before the workshop started. Now that we could access the storage room, we headed back to the school gymnasium, where it was located.

"We saw something crazy back there," I mumbled.

Yoshino and I reached the storage room and found the blackout curtain, but then we sank to the floor, too exhausted to move.

"Things sure are different from junior high, huh?"

In high school, seeing a couple wasn't uncommon. I couldn't help feeling a little envious watching boys and girls chat in the hallway during breaks between classes. Back in junior high, people usually teased couples they found out were dating, so most relationships were kept secret.

"I've heard stuff like that happens all the time in this storage room," Yoshino murmured, finally catching her breath as she sat holding the curtain.

"Really? How do you know that?" I inquired.

"There are rumors about it. Like, during festival prep, couples get the storage room key and come in here to..." Yoshino trailed off.

Just imagining what she was about to say brought heat to my cheeks. Yoshino seemed to be having the same thought; her face was beet red. We scooted close enough together to feel each other's breath. Trying to calm down, we whispered in hushed tones that were completely unnecessary given no one else was around.

"Why do you think they were by the first-year fountains, though?"

"Probably because so few people use those. If no one came by, do you think they would've..." Before I could finish my question, Yoshino and I locked eyes and squealed. We'd read enough shojo manga to know what happened next. I smacked the curtain gleefully, inhaled a cloud of dust, and started coughing.

"I wonder if that day will ever come for me," Yoshino sighed wistfully, tucking back some hair that had fallen in her face. Her skin looked paler than usual in the storage room's dim lighting. "I doubt it. I'm too scared of men." She smiled self-deprecatingly as she brushed dust off her skirt and reached out to me. "Let's get going."

"Okay," I agreed, taking her hand and standing up.

"You'll be with me forever, right, Hazuki?"

Even after leaving the storage room, we kept holding hands. As we walked side by side, the sun cast identical shadows behind us, like matching paper cutouts. We were around the same height, with hair cut the same length, wearing pleated skirts that fell to our knees. We carried mechanical pencils we'd bought together, and the same plush toy hung from our bags. We were two peas in a pod—everything about us matched perfectly. Whatever we did, Yoshino and I were always the same.

We unfolded the dust-covered curtain we'd retrieved from the storage room, only to discover a fair number of holes. Many years of use had thinned the material, and its red lining showed through in some spots. When we tested the curtain, holding it up to the sun and seeing light shine through, our group leader's face fell. In its current state, the curtain wouldn't provide the darkness necessary to preserve the atmosphere of a haunted house. We decided it'd be best to take the curtain to my house so Yoshino and I could mend it.

"Ouch!" I yelped softly as I pricked myself with a needle. "This curtain will be covered in blood by the time we're done with it."

"Are you okay?" Yoshino asked. "Maybe we should've asked the costume group to handle it."

They could've repaired the curtain in no time using one of the machines in the school sewing room, but the costume group already had a lot on their plate. Iron-on patches were another option, but those would eat into our already-limited budget. With those constraints in mind, we'd opted to hand-repair the curtain over the weekend at my house.

Yoshino came over often, and she seemed at home here. We were wearing the same skirt and blouse today, almost as if we'd planned it.

My finger was still bleeding—I must've pricked it deeper than I'd thought. However many times I wiped the blood away, it continued to seep out. I stood, pressing the wound with a tissue.

"I'm going to grab a bandage and go to the bathroom," I informed Yoshino.

"You should probably disinfect it while you're there."

Leaving her behind, I headed down to the living room on the first floor. I finished in the bathroom and was just going back upstairs when Chiaki called out from the kitchen, where he was rummaging through the fridge. "Hey, Hazuki, do we have any barley tea left?"

"You finished all the tea I made this morning. Why not brew some more?"

"You expect me to serve guests hot tea on a summer day?" Chiaki also had people from school over to do festival prep. Yoshino and I could hear their excited chatter through the thin wall separating the bedrooms. "Never mind. I'll just stop by the convenience store and pick something up there." He slipped his wallet into his pocket, looking annoyed.

"Can you get us ice cream while you're there?"

"Oh, sure, no problem," he muttered under his breath. "You're a real tyrant, you know."

He walked toward the front door. I saw several neatly arranged pairs of shoes there; it looked like he had both male and female guests.

Chiaki was just about to slip on his sandals when we were startled by a chime from the intercom informing us that someone was at the door. He opened it, letting hot, humid air rush in as a cheerful voice greeted us.

"Sorry we're late!" a boy said. "The convenience store took a little longer than we expected."

"Perfect timing, Riku!" my brother grinned.

The visitor was Tono-senpai. He was carrying a bag of plastic bottles that he handed to Chiaki. Tono-senpai wasn't alone; the girl at his side opened the bag she was holding, showing us the contents.

"We brought a bunch of snacks too," she added. "We can all eat them together."

"You didn't have to do that, Hasumi," Chiaki replied. "But it's much appreciated."

I'd never seen the girl before. When she noticed me, she gave me a brilliant smile. "You have a sister, Chiaki?"

"Hazuki's a year younger than us. She goes to our high school too."

"You and Hazuki-chan look practically identical," said the girl. "Do you hear that often?"

Chiaki paused deliberately, then replied, "All the time."

My first impression was that this girl was the endearing type. The soft, gentle way she called me "Hazuki-chan" lingered in my ears.

Tono-senpai also glanced between Chiaki and me, then commented, "Those large eyes must be part of the Sakura family DNA. Do you guys look more like your mother or father?"

"Come on, Riku. You're staring way too much," the girl—Hasumi-senpai—chided. She pulled Tono-senpai's sleeve, and he stuck his tongue out playfully. Then, as if she were his guardian, she said, "It might get a little loud when we're discussing the festival. I just want to apologize in advance."

"It's fine!" I replied. "I've got a friend over too."

"Oh, you do? In that case, take this and eat it together." she smiled and handed me a box of chocolates from her bag.

When he saw what she'd given me, Tono-senpai asked inquisitively, "Aren't those the brand-new chocolates you bought for yourself, Ichika?"

"Hush! You don't need to say that."

Apparently, they'd bought big packages of snacks to share with Chiaki's other guests, but that box of chocolates was the only one small enough for two people to finish. I tried to give it back to her, but she brushed me off, grinning and telling me it wasn't a big deal. She and Tono-senpai followed Chiaki up to his bedroom on the second floor.

Now that even more people were attending his festival-prep meeting, I heard their voices echoing as soon as I reached the second-floor hallway. When I returned to my room, I saw that Yoshino had made progress repairing the curtain.

"How's your finger, Hazuki? Are you okay?"

"Yeah, I'm fine. Sorry about all the noise from Chiaki's room. They're being pretty loud, huh?"

"Seems like even more people showed up. It sounds lively in there; they must be having a blast."

I could tell from how Yoshino tossed the curtain aside that she was probably getting bored with the repetitive work. Once she'd finished stretching both arms overhead, I handed her the box of chocolates. "Hasumi-senpai gave us these."

"Ooh! This is the new kind I've been wanting to try!"

"It is? I guess Hasumi-senpai wanted to try it too, but she let us have it."

"It's a limited-edition summer flavor. They usually get snatched up right away—they're hard to find."

Yoshino, who had a major sweet tooth, opened the box and showed me the individually packaged servings inside. She ripped one open, and we both tried a square of chocolate.

"Oh. It's mint chocolate," I remarked with a little hesitation.

"Delicious, isn't it? I love this flavor!" she exclaimed.

Chiaki hated mint chocolate, so I unconsciously avoided it, but Yoshino's dreamy smile made me think the refreshing, slightly toothpaste-like taste wasn't so terrible.

"I feel bad that they just let us have this. We should give them something in return."

We had our own collection of snacks. Yoshino put some in a small bag and stood up, her cramped body relaxing after sitting in the same position for ages. She'd been around Chiaki long enough to build up some resistance to him, so when I asked her to come with me, she agreed. We knocked on Chiaki's door.

The master of the room himself opened it. "What's up, Hazuki?"

"We wanted to give you these in return for the chocolates we got earlier."

I just planned to hand over the snacks and leave, but my brother's classmates immediately turned their attention to the new arrivals beyond the door.

"Who's that?" one asked.

"Is that your little sister?" asked another.

"Whoa. You look just like each other!"

In the blink of an eye, our senpai ushered us into the room and forced us to sit on the floor as they surrounded us. I could practically feel Yoshino trying to pull herself together as she took in the sight of all the boys.

"Are you Chiaki's sister too?" someone asked Yoshino.

"I'm Yoshino, Hazuki's friend," she replied.

"Whoa! You two look so alike, I thought you were twins."

Yoshino smiled awkwardly as the stares continued. We had the same hairstyle and clothes, so at first glance, we did look like identical twins. On closer inspection, it was easy to see that our faces were completely different, but I guess our senpai hadn't noticed that.

"What're the first years doing for the school festival?"

"Our class is making a haunted house."

"Oh! You must be in the class that's always working on scenery. It's incredible—you guys are at it every day!"

It seemed the upperclassmen were keeping an eye on what other classes were up to. As they peppered me with questions, I continued to humor them, looking for Tono-senpai. There wasn't room for him on the floor, so he was sitting on the bed.

"Hang on," he said. "Aren't you the girl I lent my sweatshirt to?"

Yoshino stiffened as he finally picked her out. None of our senpai would be aware of her fear of men. I was going to speak up and cover for her so that no one mistook her silence for rudeness, but she beat me to it.

"Um..." she began hesitantly. "Thanks for lending me your sweatshirt."

"No problem. I'm glad you didn't stain your uniform."

The exchange seemed completely normal, but I knew how much it must've taken out of her. She rushed back to my room almost like she was running away. I attempted to follow her, but our senpai refused to let me leave too.

"Let's talk a bit more about the school festival while you're here! The first-years are aiming for the top too, right?"

Individual classes—not entire grade levels—received points based on things like whether we cleaned up after ourselves while preparing and whether everyone worked together to pull off the class's plans. We also got points based on the outcome of games played during the festival and the quality of class presentations. Still, the third-years always won, no matter what. We just didn't want the first-years to end up in last place.

"What's your class doing?" I asked.

"Putting on a cross-dressing café," said one girl, an eye-catching beauty sitting in the middle of the room. "Your brother's going to dress up like a girl. You should come check it out."

"Don't tell her that, Iguchi!"

Despite living together, Chiaki and I hadn't discussed the school festival much. Now I knew why—he was avoiding the subject on purpose.

"Are all the boys dressing up?" I asked.

"Not me," said Tono-senpai. "I'm working behind the scenes."

"You should do it, Riku," the pretty girl—Iguchi-senpai—said. "You'd look so good dressed as a girl."

Tono-senpai refused with a resounding, “No thanks!”

He sat next to Hasumi-senpai, whose eyes were practically sparkling. We'd put a few of the chocolates she'd given us in the bag we'd brought over, and apparently, she'd spotted them. “What's that? It looks yummy.”

Before she could try one of the chocolates, Tono-senpai plucked it from her fingers and popped it in his mouth.

“Come on, Riku!” she protested.

“Sorry, sorry. I just thought it must be good if you were that excited to eat it.” Tono-senpai smiled and wiped cocoa butter from the corner of his mouth, but his expression darkened almost immediately. “Ew! This is mint chocolate. I hate that flavor!”

“Hey, that was the last one left—no, I don't want something you already bit into!”

They seemed so close that I felt my cheeks warm up just watching them, but everyone else appeared used to these exchanges. Chiaki even took a jab at them. “You guys are totally a couple, right?”

This just seemed to be par for the course in high school, but for some reason it reminded me of that scene Yoshino and I had witnessed at the water fountains.

I didn't think we could fix the curtain in one day, but thanks to Yoshino's efforts, we got it done by evening. When our senpai finally released me from Chiaki's room, Yoshino had already returned to sewing like her life depended on it. Even when I tried to make conversation, I only got silence in reply. She sewed without a single break until all the repairs were done.

At that point, she was covered in dust from the curtain, so she went to take a bath. As soon as she came back, she sank into her futon, likely exhausted from her frantic endeavors.

Yoshino often slept over. Her mother worked as a caregiver, and when she had an overnight shift, she apparently felt more comfortable with her daughter staying at a friend's house than being home alone. We'd purchased matching pajama sets to use whenever she stayed over, and the guest cover on her futon's duvet was the same kind as mine.

I could hear her breathe rhythmically as she slept. Turning off my bedroom lights, I headed back down to the living room.

"Huh? Where's Yoshino?"

"She fell asleep. She must've been tired from all that detail work."

"I wonder if the noise from the next room distracted her. Still, our house was the only place that worked for my group to all get together."

Fresh from the bath, Chiaki sprawled on the sofa and scrolled through his phone. When he saw me take a two-pack of push-up popsicles from the freezer, he silently reached out his hand. I split the popsicles apart and handed him one, sitting on what little space was left on the sofa.

"Do you think she ran away because she was scared of us?" he asked.

"Probably. Still, I know she wants to do something about that. All we can do for her is have her back."

Chiaki was aware of Yoshino's phobia. We'd both picked up on it from conversational tidbits she'd shared about her parents divorcing before she even remembered them being together, never having a father figure around, and subsequently developing an extreme fear of men.

"She's scared of men, but it's not like she doesn't *like* them," Chiaki mused. "Still, I feel bad for her. She won't be able to enjoy the post-festival bonfire, and that's the most exciting event."

During the festival, classes ran various booths, and clubs gave exhibitions and presentations. Once those wrapped up, a huge bonfire took place in the middle of the courtyard, and students danced to various folk songs. It was a popular school tradition passed from one generation of students to the next—and, apparently, famous for producing many couples. The classic pattern was that a boy and girl got close while prepping for the festival, which usually culminated in confessing feelings for each other at the bonfire. They'd then become an item.

"What about you? Do you have a reason to look forward to the bonfire?" I asked.

"Naw. I think I'll just boogie to the 'Mayim Mayim' in drag with the other guys."

It was easy to picture them dancing around, shouting wildly. Just the thought made me chuckle.

"If Yoshino saw me dressed as a girl, how do you think she'd react? Maybe it'd help rehabilitate her."

"Absolutely not. She'd probably just run away from you."

Chiaki continued enthusiastically tapping and scrolling on his phone as he sucked his tubular popsicle. I suspected he was participating in a group chat with the guests he'd had over earlier in the day.

"Think I could wear your clothes too, Hazuki?" he asked.

"Don't even try it. You'd rip them for sure."

Chiaki knew we had very different physiques. However close we were in age, we weren't the same sex.

"Yeah, you're right," he murmured. "Iguchi's in charge of our costumes. She mentioned there's something off about the visuals when boys wear clothes meant for girls. She says she's going to practice doing our makeup before the festival, too."

Iguchi-senpai, the stunningly pretty girl I'd seen in Chiaki's room, sometimes came up in Chiaki's conversations. I'd thought they might be dating, but given what he said about the bonfire, it seemed they didn't have that kind of relationship.

"Sounds like she's looking into whether we should use wigs or hair extensions," Chiaki continued. "She says that if we don't have the budget for them, she's willing to cover the difference herself. That won't be cheap, though."

Iguchi-senpai's light-colored hair had caught my attention. She was stunning, and I got the impression she wasn't the type to compromise on appearances in the least. If the boys were transformed under her watch, even my brother might end up looking presentable.

I finished my popsicle and got up to brush my teeth. Chiaki had been absorbed in his phone the entire chat, but he glanced over when he felt the sofa shift.

"You always wear those pajamas when Yoshino spends the night," he observed.

"What's wrong with that? This way, we match," I quipped.

The pajamas in question were cherry-blossom pink and made from lightweight cotton. I liked them so much I wouldn't have minded wearing them every night, but I only put them on when Yoshino stayed over.

Chiaki continued to study me, pouting. "Sometimes I mistake her for you at school and talk to her, you know. When I do, she looks terrified. It doesn't feel great."

Yoshino and I looked so similar, even my brother mixed us up. I knew Chiaki meant that as a complaint, but it was the best compliment he could've given me.

"You guys always dress the same," he muttered. "I just don't get the appeal of looking like twins."

He didn't say anything else after that, seemingly reabsorbed into his exciting group chat.

I brushed my teeth and returned to my room. I tried to open the door quietly, but I noticed Yoshino stir.

“Sorry. I fell asleep,” she murmured.

“Don’t worry. You did all that hard work by yourself. Go back to sleep and get some rest.” I got into bed without turning on the lights.

Yoshino seemed wide awake, though. She sat up and peered at my face. “Hey, Hazuki…”

“What’s up?”

“Was I acting strange today?”

What happened when we went to the other room must be bothering her, I thought, then repeated the concerns Chiaki had brought up earlier word for word.

“I figured I must’ve come off as awkward. I was just so nervous,” Yoshino replied.

“That’s not true. Everyone complimented you and said how cute you were.”

“Tono-senpai probably thinks I’m weird.”

To the casual observer, it would’ve seemed perfectly normal to thank someone who lent you their sweatshirt, but I knew just how much courage it took for Yoshino to initiate that conversation with Tono-senpai.

“Are Chiaki and Tono-senpai good friends?” she asked.

“Well, they’re in the same class. And they seemed to be chatting about the school festival earlier.”

Yoshino paused, then muttered under her breath, “If I go to their class during the festival, maybe I can see him.” She twisted the sheets in her fingers as she talked to herself.

Her head was angled down, so I couldn't hear her clearly. As I leaned closer to pick up on what she was saying, she suddenly looked up at me.

"Um, Hazuki… I might be okay if it's Tono-senpai."

Our faces were so close, I felt the warmth of her breath. Even in the dark, I could tell her eyes were sparkling. Her gaze was so magnetic, it felt like I was being pulled in.

"I'm scared of him, but I'm not. It's the first time I've ever felt this way about a boy," she continued. "I wonder why. Maybe because he's a little older? A high-schooler? He's not like those *other* boys at all."

I knew the true reason for Yoshino's aversion to men. Her phobia had come from being bullied as a child.

Most of the teasing stemmed from her name, Somei Yoshino, just like the cherry tree. She hadn't been born Somei, but taking her mother's maiden name after her parents divorced caused her inevitable misfortune. While people who knew the reason for her name were usually polite and didn't make comments, once Yoshino got into junior high, a boy who'd attended a different elementary started giving her a hard time about it.

The other girls didn't want to get caught up in the drama, so they started avoiding Yoshino, making her feel even more isolated. She'd transferred to my school at such a random time because that was basically when Yoshino's mother noticed a strange change in her daughter's behavior: she would completely freeze up around men.

Fortunately, no one bullied Yoshino at her new school, but all the abuse she'd experienced damaged her ability to build relationships. Everyone could tell something was a little off about her. It couldn't be denied that she was a bit of an odd duck, but that just made her unique.

Yoshino loved reading shojo manga, and she often lent them to me. We'd trade opinions on the stories, and she'd tell me she wanted to experience love like that herself someday. I was certain she still felt the same way, and that she'd like nothing more than to have that wish granted at the high school she'd worked so hard to enter.

"Do you like Tono-senpai?" I asked.

Even in the dim light, I could see Yoshino's cheeks turning pink. After a slight pause, she replied, "I don't know yet. I'm still scared of him, but my heart races whenever I see his face."

Instant palpitations sounded like a sure sign of liking someone to me, but Yoshino didn't seem certain of her budding feelings yet.

"I'd like to stop by his class during the school festival," she added. "Will you come with me, Hazuki?"

I always immediately liked the manga Yoshino liked. Due to Chiaki's influence, I'd only ever read shonen manga before, so I'd never imagined such delicate, heartwarming stories existed. If seeds of love were blossoming in Yoshino's heart, I wanted to share that experience with her.

"Okay. I'll get Chiaki to give us some café vouchers."

"Thanks!" Yoshino smiled so broadly that I caught the faint

scent of her toothpaste. It smelled just like the mint chocolate we'd eaten earlier that afternoon.

We always styled our hair the same way and wore matching outfits. We were inseparable, even at school. Having read the same manga and eaten the same sweets as Yoshino, I'd come to like shojo stories and the flavor of mint chocolate.

If Yoshino falls in love with Tono-senpai, I mused, *will I fall in love with him too?*

O

Every class period the day before the festival was used to prepare. We spent the entire day decorating the school and transforming it into an extraordinary space.

The groups in charge of haunted house costumes, small props, and gadgets were on their last sprint to the finish line. Meanwhile, those of us working on the set went all out putting up scenery in the classroom. We were using all the desks and chairs in addition to the set pieces with intriguing gimmicks we'd spent ages working on. There was something thrilling about transforming the ordinary classroom we used each day. At the same time, I was hit with the bittersweet realization that today marked the end of the long prep period.

I put set pieces together according to our group leader's instructions. As I handed him some plywood boards, he suddenly asked, "Is Somei feeling okay?"

Yoshino had a fever, so she was resting in the school infirmary. Our group leader seemed pretty worried about her. "She's fine," I replied. "I think she just overexerted herself getting everything ready for the festival."

Our group had wound up really busy with painting as we finished constructing one set piece after another. Yoshino was a skilled artist, and she really shined when it came to painting. When it was time to decorate the classroom, however, I'd noticed she seemed unsteady on her feet.

"Somei's the type who takes on a task no matter what's asked of her," the group leader reflected. "I wound up giving her a lot of work. Maybe I overdid it."

"It's just a slight fever. The nurse said she'll be fine, as long as she takes it easy today," I reassured him. I'd accompanied Yoshino to the infirmary, so I had a good idea of the situation.

Even after the classroom was ready, the scenery group had more work to do. The boys were going to handle the set's various tricks from behind the scenes while Yoshino and I, dressed like ghosts, would signal them to trigger the mechanisms.

"Is anyone you know coming to the festival?" I asked the group leader. "Seems like everyone's inviting friends or family."

My parents weren't coming. Chiaki had made it crystal clear that inviting them was off the table, since he hadn't told them he'd be cross-dressing. Yoshino and I had made plans to walk around the festival together since her mother would be working that day.

"Some guys from my junior-high baseball club said they'd come," the group leader replied.

"Where'd you go again?"

It was an innocuous question, but he paused uncomfortably before naming the junior high Yoshino had attended before transferring to this school. "I don't think Somei recognizes me," he added. "We were in different classes, and we never talked to each other."

"Why didn't you tell her?"

"I'm sure she doesn't want to be reminded of those uncomfortable memories. She was infamous—even kids in other classes knew about her."

Yoshino didn't talk about it much, but some students had shot videos of her being bullied and posted them in other classes' group chats. She'd had plenty of opportunities to see our group leader at their previous school, but he told me she tended to walk around with her head down, not looking anyone in the face.

"Seeing her again in high school, I was shocked by how different she seemed. I guess her transfer went well." He glanced at me. "Somei can't talk to guys because of what happened in junior high, right? Lately, though, she's stopped running away when I say something to her. It seems like she's recovering a little."

He was right. As festival prep progressed, I'd seen some change in Yoshino. First, she assertively started taking on tasks she'd previously done only if asked. Then she'd gotten to the point that, if she needed to ask a boy for something, she could initiate that conversation—although she'd be blushing. She also began to actively enjoy our work in the courtyard.

I knew the reason for the changes: Tono-senpai was there.

After the incident in Chiaki's room, he seemed to remember us; he'd come by and say hi while we worked in the courtyard. Occasionally, he stood nearby and watched Yoshino paint, sometimes calling others over to look at her work.

One time, Tono-senpai had yelped, "Hey, Rintaro! Come over here!" Class 2-A's homeroom teacher, Kakei Rintaro, was heading through the outdoor walkway. "You like these kinds of pictures, don't you?"

Kakei-sensei taught first-year Japanese language and literature, so his sudden appearance didn't alarm Yoshino. "Whoa. You're pretty good," he'd remarked.

He glanced around our work area. Kakei-sensei was a younger teacher, and there was still a childishness to his face. I noticed that he didn't chide Tono-senpai for speaking to him without honorifics, so that was probably par for the course in his class.

Yoshino was painting a ghostly woman wearing a white robe with disheveled black hair in a style reminiscent of a traditional Japanese painting. The corners of Kakei-sensei's slightly weary eyes crinkled as he examined it. "Is this based on the ghost in *The Dish Mansion at Bancho*?"

"Y-yes," Yoshino replied. Her hands trembled as she painted, but I knew she wasn't shaking from fear. She was nervous because Tono-senpai was watching.

He called over even more classmates, and we were surrounded in no time. "*The Dish Mansion at Bancho*?" one said. "Isn't that the story of Oiwa? The ghost who counts dishes? Like 'One... two... Oh no, there's a dish missing!'?"

"Huh? I thought Oiwa was the ghost with bruised eyes," remarked another.

"Why was Oiwa counting dishes again?" a third chimed in.

As the boys around us chattered, Kakei-sensei sighed. "Oiwa's from *Yotsuya Kaidan*. The ghost in *The Dish Mansion at Bancho* is Okiku."

"You're so cool, Rintaro!" his students chorused.

The Dish Mansion at Bancho and *Yotsuya Kaidan* were both famous stories featuring female ghosts. The feminine form Yoshino was painting on the black plywood radiated otherworldliness. She wasn't using color—just white and black—which emphasized the spooky vibe.

"Once the festival ends, why not join the art club? I'm jealous of those painting skills." Kakei-sensei, who oversaw the club, seemed very impressed.

"You're quite the artist yourself, right, Rintaro?" Tono-senpai remarked with a slight shrug.

"I'm just the official club advisor. But we do have a qualified art teacher give lessons a couple times a month. And the upperclassmen are skilled—they can teach you a lot."

Neither Yoshino nor I belonged to a club. Our school emphasized producing well-rounded students, and regulations strongly recommended that everyone participate in the extracurricular clubs on campus. Yoshino, however, worried about having to interact with boys, had chosen not to join any.

Yoshino stopped painting for a moment, looking uncomfortable. "I'm very shy," she murmured in a barely audible voice.

"Chiaki's in the art club," Tono-senpai replied matter-of-factly. "It won't be too scary if someone you know is there, right?"

"Chiaki-kun's in the art club?"

My brother was one of the very few boys Yoshino could interact with. And if someone in the club was aware of her circumstances, they'd have her back in the unlikely event something bad happened.

"Sounds perfect, doesn't it?" I said encouragingly. "Why not check it out after the festival?" I was sure new school friends would do her a world of good.

"Will you come with me, Hazuki?"

As I nodded, her tense face finally relaxed.

"I know you're first-years, but since we're all here, let me go ahead and get your names," said Kakei-sensei.

"I'm Somei Yoshino."

"I'm Sakura Hazuki."

After we introduced ourselves, Kakei-sensei chuckled. "Both a Somei Yoshino, and a North Japanese hill-cherry tree. Perfect. Sounds like you two were meant to be friends."

Yoshino and I already knew both our names were related to cherry blossoms—that was why we bought so many matching light-pink items. My surname, "Sakura," was pronounced the same way as the word for "cherry tree," although it used different kanji. I didn't understand the link to North Japanese hill cherry, though.

"Somei Yoshino leaves only grow after the trees bloom. The blossoms come in first. On the other hand, the North Japanese hill cherry grows blossoms and leaves at the same time," Kakei-sensei explained. "Just like you two, they look alike, but they're completely different trees."

The cherry trees on our campus were North Japanese hill cherry. I'd seen them bloom every year, but never noticed that the leaves and flowers sprouted at the same time. That was just something we overlooked.

I suddenly recalled that my junior-high homeroom teacher, who'd volunteered me to show Yoshino around the school, was also a Japanese literature and language arts teacher. Maybe it wasn't coincidental after all that she'd paired Yoshino and me up.

"I'll be waiting for you guys in the art room," Kakei-sensei finished.

If I check the club out with Yoshino, will they think I want to join too? I wondered.

Unlike my brother, I wasn't great at drawing. If I joined a club that bored me, I didn't know whether I could stick it out until graduation. Yoshino probably wouldn't take the plunge if I didn't do it with her, though.

After helping the group leader finish his tasks, I stopped by the infirmary to check on Yoshino. Before going inside, I knocked on the door, but the school nurse didn't seem to be around. The festival was approaching, and it seemed like everyone was busy.

I made my way over to the bed next to the window. "Are you feeling better, Yoshino?"

I spoke in a hushed whisper even though the other beds were empty. It felt like the natural thing to do when visiting the infirmary. Opening the bed's privacy curtain, I saw that Yoshino was sleeping. Her complexion looked much better than earlier. I gazed at her, breathing as quietly as possible so I wouldn't wake her.

Just before we'd finished the last tasks in our classroom, our group leader asked me, "Hey, Sakura, do you and Somei have plans for the post-festival bonfire?"

I shook my head. Yoshino and I had promised each other we'd go to all the classroom attractions and booths together, but we'd never made specific plans for the post-festival events. Still, we had a silent understanding that, whatever plans we made, we'd do them together.

"If you guys are cool with it, I wanted to get together with everyone in our group. Kind of like a wrap-up party. If after the festival doesn't work, maybe during summer break?"

His ears were turning red, but I pretended not to notice.

What would I do if Yoshino said she wanted to meet up with Tono-senpai once the festival ended? There were several ways I could help her do that, the easiest of which was just asking Chiaki. I didn't get the impression that Tono-senpai was the kind of person who would snub us.

Yoshino and I had two hearts that beat as one, and I loved what she loved. But...

"Yoshino..." I spoke her name, but my voice couldn't reach her. Leaning over, I softly kissed her lips as she murmured something unintelligible in her sleep.

The one I loved was Yoshino.

o

The school festival finally arrived. The first-years seemed almost overwhelmed by the high school event's free atmosphere; it was quite a change from the festivals in junior high, which still felt quite childish.

The festival was held over two days. On the first day, only students could visit the campus, which was hosting events like an opening ceremony, club presentations, and a band performance. The next day, the festival was open to the public, and people flocked to check out the various cafés and classroom attractions. Some schools used entry tickets to keep out visitors who might be up to no good, but not ours. Anyone could come and go as they pleased.

Class 1-C's haunted house only had a few visitors at first. It was common knowledge that school-festival haunted houses weren't great—a lot of students mockingly said as much when they first entered. Before long, however, you could hear their screams of terror echoing into the hallway. Students began to notice how haggard guests looked upon exiting, and before long, a line of people wanting to experience our haunted house began to form.

Darkness blanketed the haunted house classroom, thanks to the repaired blackout curtain and blinds we'd placed in other gaps. Visitors weren't given any lights; they had to walk through relying only on the dim glow of indirect lighting as creepy background music played. To lower their guard, the haunted house used childish pranks at the beginning. We squirted visitors with water guns and walked them through suspended chunks of konjac jelly. Once they advanced farther inside, it was time for the products of the scenery group's labor—our mechanized set pieces—to shine.

Yoshino and I took turns in the haunted house. We wore white yukata and, when someone got close, signaled the boys operating the set pieces. The unsuspecting visitor would believe nothing was there, so when a ghost suddenly appeared behind them and caught them off guard, they'd scream in terror. They'd scramble away, only to run straight into Yoshino's masterpiece, the Japanese-style painting of a ghostly woman appearing before them in a flash of light. They'd be petrified for a moment, then realize it was only a picture. Their relief was short-lived, however, since the set piece immediately revolved to reveal a real ghost clad in a white yukata directly overhead.

The haunted house would have seemed less scary if groups bumped into each other along the way, so I was standing right by the exit, monitoring the number of people leaving. By the time guests reached me, they looked completely drained—they'd probably screamed too much internally. I saw the tension in their faces melt as they neared the exit, but when I greeted them with a final "Congratulations on surviving!" they almost always squealed in terror again.

"Eeeek!" Someone shrieked so close to me, I thought it might damage my hearing.

Two students were approaching the exit—a boy whose wails nearly shattered my eardrums and the girl he was clinging to. My eyes had adjusted to the darkness, so I immediately recognized them. It was Tono-senpai and Hasumi-senpai.

"Tono-senpai?" I said.

They must've recognized me too. Tono-senpai immediately tried to look as though he hadn't been on the verge of fainting from fear just moments earlier. "Sheesh, was it really *that* scary, Ichika?" he asked casually.

"I think *you* were the one screaming your head off the whole time, Riku," Hasumi-senpai replied, mercilessly sabotaging his attempt to salvage the situation.

I had a little time before the next group would emerge, so I followed them through the exit into the hallway's dazzling light.

"Thanks for coming," I said. "Chiaki bought a bunch of haunted house tickets, so I was hoping I might see you guys."

"It was so scary!" Tono-senpai admitted. "I shouldn't have assumed it'd be like all those other high-school haunted houses."

Beads of sweat trickled down his forehead. I wanted to go get Yoshino, but she was signaling the boys in the classroom.

"Our shifts will be over soon," I told them. "Yoshino and I are planning to see your class's café after that."

"Your brother and I should both be working then," Tono-senpai replied. "He should be getting ready right now. Hope you're looking forward to seeing his moment of glory."

Chiaki was scheduled for the afternoon shift, but getting dressed and having his makeup done would apparently take a while. Hasumi-senpai and Tono-senpai, meanwhile, wore simple white shirts and black pants. "You're not cross-dressing yourself, Tono-senpai?"

"They did create an outfit for me, but I'm more comfortable dressed this way," he replied.

"Aw. That's too bad. I wanted to see you in drag." He was a little tall, but his androgynous features would probably transform him into quite an attractive girl.

A smile I couldn't quite read flashed across his face. Then he whistled softly at the raucous screams coming from within the haunted house. "Sounds like someone's having a blast in there. Anyway, we'll see you later. I'll make sure you get a free drink."

"Thanks." I watched the pair walk off together, then headed back toward the exit to see what was going on.

Just outside the haunted house, some boys were smirking and laughing as they listened to screams from within. They were probably friends of the group currently moving through the haunted house. We only allowed up to three people inside at a time, so they and their pals had likely been split into two groups.

I pulled the door open and crept back through the exit. As the screams gradually moved closer, I could easily guess which part of the haunted house they were moving through. They were probably right by Yoshino's painting.

"Gaaaaah!"

A scream that could've shattered glass rang out as a flurry of footsteps raced in my direction. There must've been a girl in the group. Judging by the sound of her footfalls, she was making her way toward me incredibly fast. My role monitoring the exit included making sure no guests tripped or fell over as they left, so I called out to ask if she was okay. However, she kept screaming as she pushed me out of the way and fled the classroom.

The impact of our collision sent me flying into some desks we were using as scaffolding. That part of the set almost collapsed, but our group leader, who was also lurking behind the scenes, noticed at the last second and kept them from tumbling over.

"You okay, Sakura?" he called.

I'd pulled part of the curtain down with me when I fell, and light from outside flooded in, illuminating the concern written all over his face.

I realized the girl who'd zoomed by me had been wearing a white yukata. "That was Yoshino just now..." I trailed off.

As I tried to figure out what was going on, the visitor group inside the haunted house screamed again, approaching the exit.

This area wasn't pitch black anymore, though, so their fear seemed to be abating quickly.

"Huh? Is that you, Captain? So, this's where you hid."

It was a group of boys. From the casual way they spoke to our group leader, I guessed they'd probably been members of his junior-high baseball team.

"We all decided to come see you," one boy added, "Since you're the only one of us who went to a different high school."

"Hey, wasn't that Somei back there?" another interjected.

At the mention of Yoshino's name, our group leader's face paled.

"It makes no sense for someone playing a ghost to scream and run off," one of the boys said mockingly. "Why didn't you tell us you were at the same high school as her?"

The boy's jeering tone immediately clicked everything into place in my head. These had to be the boys who'd bullied Yoshino at her previous junior high. She'd been waiting in the classroom to give the signal whenever visitors walked by, so her eyes would've been accustomed to the dark. She'd probably gotten a clear view of the group, recognized the faces of the boys who'd tortured her so horribly, and started screaming.

"Yoshino!" I yelled after her, starting to chase her along the crowded hallway. I was still dressed as a ghost, and I could feel the surprised looks I got as I dashed past everyone.

Yoshino, however, had already disappeared from sight. In her agitated state, she'd likely just run in a straight line. Following her presumed path, I ended up in the second-year area. It was a little scary because I could feel the upperclassmen's suspicious gazes burning into me. Another scream sent me dashing toward Class 2-A, where the hallway came to a dead end.

I heard a familiar voice beyond the screams. "Yoshino, what's wrong? It's me, Chiaki."

Chiaki looked about halfway ready for his café shift. He wore a deep-red dress, but his makeup still wasn't finished. He'd stopped Yoshino's frenzied escape and grabbed both her flailing hands, but Chiaki restricting her movements seemed to panic Yoshino even more.

A crowd started to form in the hallway. As students hemmed and hawed about whether to call a teacher, I caught sight of a tall figure making his way through the spectators.

Yoshino summoned all her remaining strength to break free from Chiaki's grasp. She still seemed to be in a state of utter confusion, waving her arms wildly and leaving scratch marks on her face. Then someone called her name and grabbed her hands to keep her from injuring herself. It was Tono-senpai, with Hasumi-senpai not far behind him. They must've recognized me darting frantically past them in my yukata and realized something was wrong.

"Yoshino!" I yelped her name as I threw my arms around my friend. My heart felt like it was going to explode in my chest from running full tilt, but that sensation paled in comparison to the pain I felt hearing her anguished moans.

"It's going to be okay, Yoshino. It's going to be okay." I rubbed her back, trying my best to comfort her, but she was breathing erratically, and she fainted in my arms.

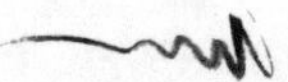

A group of teachers who'd heard the commotion helped diffuse the situation. They took Yoshino to the infirmary since the school nurse was on duty and would ensure she got appropriate care. I tried to go with her, but they rebuffed me: "We can take it from here. Just go back and finish your shift."

We closed the haunted house temporarily to fix the damaged section of the set. By the time our repairs were done, it was time for the afternoon shift to take over. I wanted to visit Yoshino and see how she was doing, but the group leader and I had received word that the second-years wanted to see us.

They're probably upset because we caused that uproar, I thought, nervously following the classmate of Chiaki's who'd come to take us to Class 2-A.

Walking through the classroom curtains, we found ourselves in a dimly lit interior. It shone with a pink glow interspersed with colorful splashes of an indirect neon glimmer. The lighting filled the classroom with a nightclub-like atmosphere that seemed almost inappropriate for high school.

"Come here, Hazuki," a voice called out way in the back, and I spotted a completely transformed Chiaki. Smoky eyes peeked out from under his wavy wig's long bangs. The makeup overemphasized his features; it was more like stage makeup than what a normal girl wore. His lipstick—deep red, to match his dress—was slathered on just like a Hollywood actress's, but it balanced out his large eyes well. He sat cross-legged, and a shapely, completely hairless leg peeked through the high slit that ran up his skirt.

Looking around the classroom, I noticed all the boys cross-dressing wore similar garish clothes and makeup. Some purposely showed off their muscular physiques, while others forewent wigs altogether, sporting their usual short hair. "This is...incredible, Chiaki."

My brother's bright-red lips curled into a smile at my impulsive remark. "We went for a drag-queen look instead of copying girls we knew. Don't we look fabulous?"

Even his tone was high-pitched. I had a feeling he'd decided to go all-in once he knew no one else in our family was coming. Even his flirty gestures were on point—he must've spent a lot of time rehearsing and getting into character.

"These little guys seemed to be just itching to leave," Chiaki drawled. "So, the *girls* and I made sure to take special care of them."

He was referring to a group seated around a table at the very back of the classroom. I recognized them as the boys from my group leader's junior high. They'd gotten a huge kick out of watching the incident with Yoshino unfold, even going as far as taking pictures of the ensuing chaos. When teachers showed up, they'd tried to flee the scene, but Chiaki and his friends stopped them first.

The boys appeared pale and shrunken as the glamorous drag queens surrounded their table. Tono-senpai was in the mix too—his slicked-back hair and black suit and tie looked especially intimidating.

"Since you so kindly joined us, why not at least stay for a drink? It may not look like it, but we don't serve alcoholic beverages."

"Perhaps these little kids would like sweet warm milk or something?"

"We've got quite the show prepared. I do hope you're looking forward to it."

The Class 2-A boys seemed almost giddy with delight. It was hard to believe they were only a year older than our group leader's friends, who looked like small children in comparison. Tono-senpai noticed my yukata loosening, and he gave me his jacket to cover myself before disappearing somewhere.

"So, boys, how do you know Yoshino?" Chiaki continued.

"We just went to the same junior high. It's not a big deal," one replied. "It isn't like we came here for her anyway. We just wanted to see our old baseball team captain."

"These guys weren't invited in the first place!" a different boy protested. "They just started tagging along out of nowhere!"

The guys from the baseball team were already throwing each other under the bus. They squabbled like whining puppies until a single glare from Chiaki silenced them.

"All right," he said. "It isn't fair to keep anyone here who wasn't involved. If that's the case, you're free to leave."

At Chiaki's prompting, the boys our group leader had actually invited rose from the table and walked away. As they passed their former captain, I heard them apologize; all he gave them in return was a silent nod. He knew exactly what had happened in Yoshino's past; I was confident he hadn't invited any of her bullies.

Only three boys remained—the same three in the group that had encountered Yoshino. They were apparently also the ones who'd snapped pictures from the crowd afterward.

"First off," said Chiaki, "how about you delete those pictures?"

"We didn't take any."

"Don't you lie to me!" Chiaki bellowed threateningly.

That seemed to do the trick. Looking terrified, one boy showed my brother his phone. I saw a snapshot of me cradling Yoshino. Her yukata was open, revealing her legs and a glimpse of her undershirt. He must've had his finger on the shutter the whole time; the entire camera roll was full of similar pictures.

"Did you upload any of these?"

"No."

"Did you send any to a group chat?"

"No."

Chiaki and the other second-year boys examined the phone.

Thankfully, it seemed like they'd captured the troublemakers before they distributed any photos. The upperclassman deleted the images one after another.

Then, grimacing, Chiaki watched a video they'd taken. Yoshino's screams echoed through the hallway as I desperately gave chase, calling after her. Our voices mixed with peals of laughter from the cameraman. There was no doubt about it—these had to be the boys who'd bullied Yoshino in junior high.

"Since you deleted all the photos, can we go now?" one boy asked brazenly, seeming completely calm and collected. "It's not like we go to this school, so we won't see her again. That's good enough, right?"

The malicious laughter in their video kept ringing in my ears. Just hearing it quickly conjured images of the torture Yoshino must've experienced all those years.

"Why did you bully her?" I couldn't help but ask.

"No real reason. It was just a way to kill time," he answered nonchalantly.

At that moment, Tono-senpai returned carrying a tray of drinks. He silently set glasses of water in front of the boys, then returned to where Chiaki and his other classmates sat.

"I know this wasn't always the case, but these days, you get in serious trouble for bullying," Tono-senpai said. "Didn't you think about the consequences to yourselves?"

"It's not like my parents could do anything about it," the boy replied.

"Why would you say that?" Tono-senpai asked calmly, keeping his emotions in check.

The boy heaved a big sigh. "Because Somei and I are siblings."

I was so taken aback, I couldn't help butting in. "What'd you just say?"

"To be more specific, we're half-siblings. We both take after our moms, so we don't look much like each other. We definitely have the same dad, though."

His unexpected confession silenced the entire room—us and his own friends alike.

He was still using the same nonchalant tone, but I spied his feet tapping nervously under the table. "It didn't seem like Somei had a clue, but I overheard Dad discussing it with my mom one night while they looked at a student list for my class. I never knew Dad was on his second marriage until then."

"Why would that make you bully her?" I pressed.

"Why? Because *I'm* the victim here. I was shocked to learn my dad was divorced. Plus, I was pissed that they hid the fact I had a sibling from me."

Our group leader mumbled the boy's name under his breath. The bully's surname was common, so unless she knew his full name already, Yoshino's mother probably wouldn't have realized he was her ex's son—not even if she saw a class list.

Yoshino had suffered horrible bullying without even knowing why. This boy had traumatized her until she was too terrified even to speak in front of men, and the mere sight of his face had sent her into a panic.

"The school called my parents in after Somei transferred, but Dad didn't say anything. At home, we just pretend she doesn't exist. What's wrong with that?"

He seemed so unapologetic. I was completely dumbfounded.

Yoshino had always longed for a sibling. She often mentioned how jealous she was of Chiaki and me, how maybe her life would've been different if she grew up with a brother. And yet, here he was, the flesh-and-blood brother she'd always longed for was the one who'd caused her so much anguish.

No one in the room knew what to say after the boy's shocking revelation. His expression turned triumphant as he took in our stunned reactions.

Tono-senpai broke the long silence. "So, that's how it went down. Thanks for putting your cards on the table."

He started to hand the bully's phone back, but just before the boy took it, Tono-senpai let go. The phone splashed into a glass of water, and the boy gave a small yelp, leaning to fetch it out.

But Tono-senpai grabbed his collar and pulled him close. "You, the victim?" he whispered. "Don't make me laugh. The one you should be upset with is your own father. Yoshino didn't do anything wrong."

The bully kept glaring at Tono-senpai, although the color drained quickly from his face. "That girl was just coming to school without a care in the world. She didn't have a damn clue."

"If it bothered you so much, why didn't you tell her what was going on? I'm guessing you stayed silent because you felt inferior to her, huh?" Tono-senpai was dressed like a bouncer, but there was something almost feminine about the way he was talking. Maybe the glitzy café atmosphere was affecting him too.

Since this boy and Yoshino were in the same school year, their mother's pregnancies—and other interactions with their father—must've overlapped. If word of their father's dalliances got out, it wasn't out of the question that people would spread rumors about the man's son. Neither child was to blame for their parents' actions, but this boy couldn't deny that he was the product of his father's affair.

"Did you bully Yoshino because you were scared of being bullied yourself?" Tono-senpai whispered in the boy's ear.

He seemed to have the bully's motives completely figured out; the younger boy's pale face flushed red instantly.

"You sorry excuse for a man," Tono-senpai snapped. He released the boy's collar and watched as he tumbled to the ground and then sat back up on the floor. "Go back home and suck your mommy's tits," Tono-senpai seethed at the boy, with a coldness in his eyes I'd never seen before.

Yoshino, my heart cried out her name. *Yoshino, the one you love is protecting you.*

o

Not many people heard about that incident, and the post-festival celebration went on without a hitch.

The window by Yoshino's infirmary bed had a great view of the bonfire. As the group leader and I discussed what had happened with Yoshino, she just silently stared out into the schoolyard.

"I'm really sorry. I never should've invited those guys from junior high," our group leader apologized.

"You didn't do anything wrong," I said.

"And I should never have hidden the fact that we attended the same school in the first place," he added. "I'm so sorry."

"Like I said, you didn't do anything wrong," I insisted. "There's nothing you need to apologize for."

Yoshino remained silent as our group leader, and I went back and forth. She had recovered physically, but the memories of her first school festival had been horribly marred. Our group leader seemed full of remorse about his involvement in the events.

"I can take care of things from here," I told him. "Go back and join everyone else."

"But..." he protested.

"Yoshino can't go home until she gets changed," I reminded him.

I had put my school uniform back on, but Yoshino was still wearing her yukata. The group leader seemed to grasp what I was getting at, and he finally left the infirmary.

The class rankings were announced at the conclusion of the festival. Most years, the first-years just did whatever they could to avoid ending up in last place. Since Class 1-C's haunted house had been so well received, though, our year was awarded second place. Still, I couldn't help feeling mixed emotions, knowing we'd robbed Chiaki and his classmates of that crown.

The students dancing around the bonfire were mostly third-years, with some second-years joining in. Most first-years looked on from the sidelines, still too embarrassed to take part. Several Class 2-A boys dancing around were still in drag. As I watched their merrymaking, I felt like I was witnessing a school legend's birth.

Yoshino and I were still sitting there, watching the schoolyard in silence, when a figure suddenly peeked in the infirmary window and tapped the glass. The scent of burning wood flooded in with the outside air as I unlocked and opened the window.

Chiaki poked his face through. "How are you doing, Yoshino? If you feel up to it, why not come join us for a bit? The post-festival celebration is going to wrap up soon."

"...You look beautiful, Chiaki." It was the first thing Yoshino had said all night.

Chiaki was still dressed for his café shift, but his makeup was coming off from all that intense dancing. He gave a small sigh of relief as Yoshino finally spoke, his face breaking into smile. "Honestly, being dressed and made up like this is cramping my style. I feel much more comfortable in my usual clothes."

"Could've fooled me," I quipped. "You certainly seem to be having a good time."

"You better not breathe a word of this to Mom and Dad, Hazuki."

As if to emphasize Chiaki's warning, the first chords of the jenkka—a Finnish folk dance—filled the air.

Chiaki seemed to sense why Yoshino was staring past him and into the schoolyard. "Riku was worried too," he added. "I'm sure he's out there dancing somewhere. You should join us. I know he'd be relieved to see you feeling better."

Yoshino teared up at just the mention of Tono-senpai's first name. "He must think I'm so weird..."

"That's not true," Chiaki said reassuringly. "I wish you could've seen how cool he was."

Chiaki saw Yoshino as another little sister, but she'd had way fewer interactions with Tono-senpai. Still, out of everyone in the classroom, he'd been her most impassioned defender.

"I've never seen him that worked up before," Chiaki continued. "He must've been furious about what those boys did to you."

"I'm so sorry I ruined your café," Yoshino said through tears as Chiaki stroked her head. She probably didn't like the fact that he was touching her. Although she'd dredged up some tolerance for Chiaki, he was still a boy. She made no move to push his hand away, though.

Chiaki and I waited silently until Yoshino collected herself. The students outside lined up as the jenkka played. The drag queen group—who couldn't be missed, thanks to their eye-catching appearance—happened to pass right by the infirmary.

"What're you doing over there, Chiaki?" they called to him.

My brother turned to acknowledge his fellow drag queens, and they started weaving and winding their way over to us.

"Oh, is she awake now?" one asked.

"How are you feeling?" another asked Yoshino. "You didn't get hurt anywhere, did you?"

"Once you feel better, come dance with us!"

Yoshino's eyes grew big as saucers as they took in the glamorous drag queens. She hadn't been party to anything that had happened at the cross-dressing café. Seeing her expression of pure surprise, the queens struck poses.

"If anything happens, we've got your back," one drawled.

"Just remember, the boys in Class 2-A are nice, okay?"

"Of course, if you'd rather keep it between us girls, we can make that work too," another drag queen said, blowing Yoshino a kiss that made her giggle.

When we visited the classroom café, I hadn't noticed that these were the same classmates Chiaki had hosted at the festival-prep meeting in his room. I even recognized some of them from the group that had gathered to admire Yoshino's painting. Our senpai always seemed to be looking out for us, even without my realizing it.

I still vividly recalled how they'd stood up for Yoshino at the café. I'd never seen a group of people look so beautiful and strong at the same time. If only she'd been there to witness it too.

The queens pulled Chiaki into their ranks again, then danced their way back to the students circling the bonfire.

As the students did one folk dance after the next, the single cherry tree by the infirmary almost seemed to watch over them. The light of the flames dyed its leaves crimson, and the fireworks going off in the breeze made the tree appear full of cherry blossoms.

The fireworks illuminated Yoshino's profile, and she turned away to hide her red, puffy eyes. "Once the festival's done, I'll check out the art club."

"I'll go with you," I said.

She shook her head. "You shouldn't have to if you're not interested. I'm always causing you problems, Hazuki."

No, you're not. I stuck with Yoshino through thick and thin because I wanted to.

"As long as people like our senpai are around, I can push myself a little harder," she added.

You don't have to do that, I wanted to protest, but swallowed the words before they escaped my lips. Instead, I said, "I'll go grab your clothes. Let's head home together," and left the infirmary, unable to look Yoshino in the face.

The quickest way from the infirmary to the first-year classrooms was up a staircase mostly used by second-years. I wouldn't normally have chosen that route, but all the students were outside around the bonfire, so I figured no one would see me.

It seemed the windows were open, since I heard music floating in. The jenkka had ended, and I could make out the beginning of the next song, "Mayim Mayim." Chiaki and his friends were probably having a blast dancing to it at that very moment.

When I reached the top of the stairs, I was greeted by the sight of the deserted booths and attractions. The contrast between the crowds earlier and the currently empty classrooms was striking, almost as if the festival had been an elaborate dream.

The hallway lights were off, but light from the schoolyard shone through the window, so it wasn't dark. The classrooms were still decked out in their extraordinary decorations. I felt an unfamiliar pang of loneliness when I realized it wouldn't be long before they would be taken down. The two days of the festival had passed in the blink of an eye. Chiaki had told me the festival prep was the best part, and he was right.

As I walked along, trying to savor the final moments of the festive atmosphere, I spotted a couple of people inside Class 2-A. The curtains were open, and it looked like someone had already started tidying as the desks were lined up in rows. The two figures in the classroom had their backs to me. They stood near the window, gazing out over the schoolyard, and I couldn't help feeling captivated by the sight of them.

I couldn't make out their faces, due to the backlight, but both had long hair. One was a girl in a school uniform, and the other was likely a boy. He seemed to be wearing a costume, and he gave off an elegance, unlike Chiaki and the other boys. Practically pressed against each other, the two listened to the "Mayim Mayim" dancers' raucous shouts, which were clearly audible inside. I knew I shouldn't watch the pair, but I couldn't seem to tear my eyes away.

The song finally ended, and "Turkey In The Straw" began. We'd learned the folk dances that would play at the festival bonfire in P.E., but this one required girls to hold hands with boys, so Yoshino couldn't do it. Still, if the events in the haunted house hadn't transpired, she'd probably be out there now, dancing with other girls.

I needed to hurry and make my way to our classroom. Just as I was about to leave, however, the two students I'd been watching clasped hands and started to dance. Despite the jaunty melody, they moved slowly, almost like they were dancing to a ballad. Their faces remained hidden until the girl twirled, giving me a better angle to make out her features.

It was Hasumi-senpai. So, the boy by her side was...

"Tono-senpai," I mumbled to myself.

For some reason, instead of the black suit he'd worn in the classroom earlier, he now wore a thick black wig and a white cocktail dress that perfectly accentuated his slender build. Unlike Chiaki and his friends' gaudy stage makeup, Tono-senpai's makeup was soft and delicate, just like what a normal girl would wear. And, strangely, nothing seemed off about it.

They didn't dance very long. Hasumi-senpai reached out to stroke Tono-senpai's cheek and whisper something in his ear. For a moment, he looked like he was on the verge of tears. Then they kissed passionately, as if trying to consume each other.

I couldn't watch any longer. I crept away to Class 1-C, trying to keep my footsteps as light as possible. I finally understood Yoshino's attraction to Tono-senpai. When the other boys tried wearing women's clothes, they were obviously cross-dressing, but Tono-senpai was indistinguishable from the real thing. Yoshino must've sensed the feminine energy he exuded, even dressed in his normal school uniform. Still, that didn't change the fact that she'd fallen for Tono-senpai, a boy.

Our classroom was still set up as a pitch-black haunted house. I pulled the blackout curtain back partway to look for our belongings, which gave me a view of what was happening in the schoolyard below. Some wood in the bonfire exploded, and sparks flew all the way to the second floor.

All our classmates had put their things in one corner of the classroom, and thanks to our matching keychains, I easily found my and Yoshino's bags. At that point, I knew I needed to head back to the infirmary, but for some reason, I froze.

Yoshino and I had the same keychains and stationary sets in our customary cherry-pink color. From our uniforms to our hairstyles and our identical outfits, we were supposed to be two hearts beating as one. However similar we looked, though, our hearts had to be separate. After all, Yoshino and I didn't love the same person.

The flames dyed the trees crimson, and the fireworks floating in the air looked just like cherry blossom petals scattering in the wind.

Yoshino and I weren't the same at all. I'd adopted her hairstyle and her favorite color as my own. I'd convinced myself I liked shojo manga and mint chocolate, just like she did. Yet however hard I tried to match Yoshino, and however much I cared about her, we were still different people.

I'd fallen in love with Yoshino, but she hadn't fallen in love with me, and my chest throbbed painfully with the knowledge that my feelings would never be returned. The melody of "Sakura, Sakura" played over and over in my head.

Oh, how I wanted to dance with Yoshino.

PART 3

Moon Light, Moon Bright

Riku Can't Be a Goddess

"I HAD THIS DREAM. I sat with my arms folded by the side of a bed where a woman lay on her back. She quietly told me she was going to die."

The first lines from Natsume Soseki's *Ten Nights' Dreams* played through my mind as I loosened the tie of the man sleeping on the bed. A masculine odor wafted from his shirt collar. I got a whiff of the scent—which wasn't by any means unpleasant—as I sat atop him, straddling his stomach. My hair dangled into his face, and he turned his head as if it tickled him.

"Come on, get up," I said.

I received only a few unintelligible murmurs in response. An empty beer can lay toppled over on the table. He'd still try drinking them, even though he was a total lightweight—one can of beer was all it took to send him into a drunken stupor.

"Wake up, Rintaro." I tried again but got no response.

Patience running thin, I put all my weight on his stomach. He croaked like a frog being crushed and finally opened his eyes.

The first words out of his mouth sounded annoyed. "You're here *again*, Iguchi?"

At school, he gave a youthful, almost boyish impression. Seeing him here in his room, though, he looked just like a drunk middle-aged man.

Through the half-drawn navy curtains, I saw the moon drifting in the sky. The curtains blocked the unsightly streetlights and power lines, and there was something almost picturesque about the moon floating alone in the starless night sky.

"I hung your suit up for you. It would've gotten wrinkled otherwise."

The first thing you'd see upon entering his apartment were the shoes he'd haphazardly kicked off in the entryway. He'd removed his socks and tossed them on the floor with his bag, then left his suit crumpled in a pile somewhere along the way. Heading straight to the fridge, he'd grabbed a beer and downed it immediately. Before long, the alcohol went straight to his head, and he'd tumbled into bed with his limbs outstretched like a giant starfish before falling fast asleep. It was just too easy to picture that exact sequence of events.

"I put a few outfits together for you in the closet," I told him.

"Why keep sticking your nose where it doesn't belong?"

"We're embarrassed that our homeroom teacher wears the same outfit every day," I retorted.

He always put on the same tie; he found it too troublesome to search for anything that wasn't close at hand. He was a single guy living alone, but it was almost unbelievable that Kakei Rintaro, one of our school's most popular teachers, was such a slob.

"Get off," he said. "You're heavy."

Still dizzy with intoxication, he held his head in one hand, searching for a cup on the table with the other. It was just out of his reach, and I decided to tease him a bit. While still straddling him, I leaned close to his face; I could feel his breath and smell the trace of alcohol that lingered on it.

I was about to kiss him when he put a hand over my mouth. "Do that with someone you like."

"But I like *you*, Rintaro."

Instead of attempting to argue, he sat up. The momentum sent me tumbling off the bed. He must've been incredibly thirsty because he downed the water almost instantly. That seemed to give him some self-possession; he finally met my gaze. "How many times have I told you not to come here?"

"It's your fault for never changing where you hide your key."

He rose from the bed and unsteadily put on the sweatpants he usually wore around the house. Then he pulled off his collared shirt and tossed it to the floor, keeping on only the undershirt beneath. He gave a big yawn and scratched his stomach lightly. I saw his belly button poke out as he did, but he didn't have any unnecessary fat.

"Go home. Your parents are probably worried about you," he said.

"I highly doubt they even care."

Rintaro looked disgusted by my stubborn attempt to stay at his place. His true nature was curt, but he played the role of the wide-eyed, pleasant fledgling teacher at school; very few people knew his true self.

He grabbed another beer from the fridge. When he cracked it open, it made a refreshing sound. His Adam's apple bobbed as he chugged it in one gulp. Something about the sweat-drenched hair around the nape of his neck exuded unspoken sexuality.

His place wasn't big at all—just a studio apartment. The navy curtains and coffee-colored bedclothes were plain, and laundry always seemed to be scattered here and there. It wasn't clean or pretty by any stretch of the imagination. Still, I felt right at home in this bachelor pad.

After summer vacation, the classroom for 2-A returned to normal; all traces of the festival atmosphere were completely gone. I slipped inside with moments to spare.

The boy who sat beside me, Sakura Chiaki, lifted his head as I tossed my bag on my desk. He must've been sleeping—his shirt had left impressions on his face. "Morning, Iguchi."

"Good morning."

He was the only classmate I greeted. We usually exchanged post-summer-vacation pleasantries like "Oh, you got so tan!" and

"How have you been?" with people we hadn't seen for a while on the same day as the second-semester opening ceremony.

The bell rang, and Rintaro opened the door. We all stood at Chiaki's command.

Stand up. Bow. Say good morning. Every day began in the same way.

The students replied indifferently as Rintaro took attendance. His voice echoed brightly through the classroom, in contrast with their apathetic responses. He wore one of the ensembles I'd put together for him. Some girls started whispering as they noticed the light-blue striped shirt and pink tie I'd chosen.

"Looks like Rintaro's fashion sense improved," I heard one mutter. I patted myself on the back internally.

"Sakura Chiaki."

"Here," Chiaki responded, trying to suppress a yawn. He probably wasn't getting enough sleep; his charmingly large eyes looked like they would close at any moment. "Hey, Iguchi," he murmured, still rubbing his eyes, "can I see your English homework?"

"You were supposed to do that over summer vacation. Why didn't you finish it?"

"I was really busy with art club every day. Please? I'll treat you to something later to make up for it." He clasped his hands together as if he were praying.

Heaving a small sigh, I started searching for the homework folder I'd put in my desk.

Rintaro was already starting the girls' roll call. "Iguchi Hikaru."

"Here."

Rintaro checked my name off casually on his roster. He read the morning announcements, then his face broke into a nihilistic smile. "2-A's hair and uniform inspection is today. I'm sure you must be raring to go."

Once summer vacation ended, they always conducted the hair and uniform inspection the day after the school's opening ceremony. Homeroom teachers would join the second-year head teacher and guidance counselor as they went from classroom to classroom, checking each student's appearance. Our school was usually so lax that everyone almost forgot the rules; teachers only came down hard on us on inspection days.

A chorus of boos met Rintaro's suggestion that we get ready now.

"It's not like anyone sprang this on you," he pointed out. "You all knew this was coming. You should've come to school prepared."

"You say that, Rintaro, but you've still got bedhead yourself," someone retorted.

"No way." Rintaro tried to tidy the back of his hair. He'd been conscientious about what he saw head-on in the mirror, but apparently hadn't noticed his almost-artistic back cowlick until now. "I'm going to go put some water on it," he said. He disappeared from the classroom, looking more like a fellow student than our teacher.

Chiaki followed the school dress code to the letter daily, since he was our class representative, and so while the other class members fussed with their appearance, he attempted to hastily copy my homework. He wrote so fast that the hand holding his mechanical pencil blurred. I was just fastening my dark-green uniform tie when he asked out of the blue, "Does my uniform look weird anywhere?"

"No. Want to borrow my perfume, though?"

"If I did that, I'd attract more unnecessary attention."

He'd finished copying the paper, so I leaned over to retrieve it. "You smell like oil, though. Did you hole up in the art room again?"

My comment prompted him to sniff at his uniform. "Shoot. I think it absorbed some of the smell." He looked drained. I was sure he'd gotten to the art room in the early morning.

"Refresh my memory—what's the school code say about *stinking*?"

"Perfume would be too strong, though," Chiaki insisted, then called, "Hey, anyone have spray deodorant?"

"I do!"

It was Tono Riku who'd responded, which prompted Chiaki to chuckle. "Why do *you* have that?" he teased.

"It's Ichika's. And what the heck? If you laugh at me, you can't borrow it."

"My bad, my bad. Can I use it, Hasumi-san? Pretty please!" he wheedled until Tono-kun sprayed him with it.

Hasumi Ichika had even had the feminine foresight to pour some deodorant spray into a portable bottle and bring it in.

Well, color me impressed. Tono-kun had just finished dousing Chiaki with it when Rintaro reentered the classroom, the head teacher and guidance counselor in tow.

The hair and uniform inspection consisted of the teachers lining students up by the window three at a time, then checking whether their appearance conformed with the school dress code. The boys underwent a detailed examination of the length of their facial hair and the hairline around the nape of their neck.

As the head teacher approached Chiaki, his eyebrows twitched. "Are you wearing perfume, Sakura?" That elicited peals of laughter from the class, who knew exactly what had transpired.

"It's deodorant spray! I was worried that I smelled like paint!" Chiaki tried desperately to explain, but the head teacher—who was in charge of P.E.—didn't seem to buy it. It *was* true that the spray Hasumi-san had lent Chiaki smelled more like sweet air freshener.

Rintaro piped up. "Sir, Sakura's in the art club. They have a big competition soon, so he's spending a lot of time in the art room. He was probably concerned about the smell."

The head teacher paused. "I see. You're the club advisor, correct?"

He moved on to the next student; Rintaro's explanation must've done the trick. Chiaki sighed in relief while Tono-kun clasped his hands together apologetically.

Once the boys' inspection was done, it was time for the girls'. We were called in order by student number, and mine was over quickly and painlessly. A female teacher was always present for the inspections since they often required a close look at the girls' skirt length. Many girls rolled their waistband to shorten the garment, which gave the fabric odd wrinkles.

"Weren't you told to redye your hair, Manabe?"

When we were first-years, my classmate Manabe had quickly put herself on the inspection blacklist by dyeing her hair. Even if you only lightened your hair once, the color would still fade after you dyed it back. The inspections took place by the window so the teachers could get a good look at our hair in the sunlight.

"I dyed it black, just like you told me."

"It still looks brown."

"I can't help that. I lightened it before, so it's fading."

"Dyeing your hair was against the school dress code in the first place," the head teacher replied. "If it won't stay black, you need to cut it short."

Manabe didn't accept his comment without a fight. "Why keep picking on me? Hikaru's hair is lighter than mine!" she shrieked, pointing in my direction.

Her outburst caused a hush to fall over the classroom. I was fully Japanese, but I'd been born with light coloring. My eyes were chestnut, and so was my hair. It was also thin and easily damaged. The longer it grew, the more it faded, so it looked pretty light, especially in the sun.

"That's Iguchi's natural hair color," said the head teacher. "She turned in proof when she started school here."

We could apply for permission to attend school with light or curly hair if we proved it was natural—for instance, by submitting pictures of ourselves as children. Manabe and I were in the same class last year, so she should already have known that I hadn't lightened my hair.

"The school code says our hair has to be black, though. Why not make her dye it?" Manabe countered.

"Yeah," another girl chimed in. "Everyone thinks it's unfair that only *she* gets to look like that."

Other girls joined Manabe's protest. As the number of dissenters grew, I saw the teachers exchange glances.

"You teachers always play favorites with Hikaru. It's not fair!"

Just before summer vacation, during the school festival—which was supposed to bring classmates even closer together—I'd found myself squeezed out of Manabe's inner circle. Our class had opted to do a cross-dressing café, and I joined the costume group with Manabe and some of her friends. I wound up being appointed group leader. Between ordering fabric for costumes and haggling over the café budget with other groups, that time turned out way busier than I could ever have imagined.

Manabe liked secondhand clothing, and she had the sewing skill to alter things herself, so she ended up my partner in crime. We'd look for patterns and comb through magazines together, debating what would work. One day, though, I went looking for Manabe so we could talk about some of the dresses, and I found her outside with Chiaki and the rest of the scenery group.

She was the only girl in the group, a lone flower surrounded by the boys.

"I don't mind if you want to lend us a hand, but aren't you working on costume group stuff?" Chiaki was asking her.

"It's fine. I told them I was coming out here to get your measurements. I mean, it's kind of ridiculous how Hikaru suddenly changed all the costumes anyway. It's just a school festival. It's not like we need to put in that much effort..."

Manabe trailed off as Chiaki tapped her on the shoulder. Noticing my presence, she immediately fell silent.

That night, I sent an announcement to the costume team's group chat. *"Since our group got such a late start, I need everybody to focus on their costuming tasks rather than helping any other group."*

Soon after, I got a direct message from Manabe: *"If you had a problem with what I did, you should've come and talked to me yourself."*

When I replied, she just left me on read.

The festival finally arrived, and the worst-case scenario happened: our cross-dressing café lost to the first-years' haunted house. Manabe and I hadn't exchanged a word since then, and the girls she hung out with had ostracized me too. Manabe and her friends were at the top of the class food chain, so the other 2-A girls also started to keep me at arm's length. Summer vacation had come and gone, but the way I was being treated hadn't changed one bit.

I'd been standing back, quietly observing the commotion my classmates were causing, and everyone's eyes shot in my direction as I broke my silence. "It's against the school code to color your hair, so I'd break it by dyeing my hair black, wouldn't I? It'd be the same as any of you changing your hair color." I tried to keep my tone light as I glanced toward the same head teacher who'd approved my hair and uniform just a few minutes earlier. "This is my natural hair color. Do I have to dye it just so it matches everyone else's?"

The head teacher pressed his lips together tightly, but he said nothing. I stood there, waiting for his answer, but none came.

As impatience got the better of me, I sighed softly. "Whatever. I'm out of here."

Grabbing my bag, I walked out of the classroom. Chiaki called after me, but I ignored him and let the door shut behind me.

I'd struggled with insecurity about my hair since childhood. My mom had gotten pregnant with me in high school, and my father and his family moved to a town far away before I was born. I'd only seen his face in photos; he probably didn't even know the sex of his own child.

It'd be giving my mother far too much credit to say she worked as hard as she could to raise me as a single parent after that. She went through one rocky relationship after another, and my last name changed more times than I cared to count. I hated having to explain the situation to my friends each time that happened.

"Was your real dad foreign, Hikaru-chan?"

Since I'd been born with light-brown hair and eyes, I was barraged with thoughtless questions like that all the time. My friends might've asked out of mere jealousy over my appearance, but I'd never forget overhearing my own grandparents whispering about the same thing late at night. However westernized Japanese people were becoming, no one around me had such light hair.

Back in junior high, one boy in my class had actually complimented me. "Your hair's so cool, Iguchi."

We'd been smack in the middle of puberty, a period when boys and girls rarely interacted, but he was a popular kid who'd gotten along with everyone.

At the time, my female classmates were spreading rumors that I dyed my hair. I guess having a Japanese-looking face but lighter hair and eyes didn't seem believable. However many times I denied their accusations, no one believed me. That boy was the only one who believed me.

A lot of girls in my class didn't like that I was friendly with him.

When we came back after a junior-high summer vacation, one girl showed up with lightened hair. "Iguchi-san has brown hair, so we should be allowed to dye ours too," she said.

From that point on, they started coloring their hair, one after another. It wound up becoming a big problem at school. Eventually, the girls who'd lightened their hair—and me—were called to the staff room and told, "You all need to redye your hair black."

"This is my natural hair color," I'd protested.

"You need to dye yours too, Iguchi. School rules state that everyone needs black hair."

What the staff were asking seemed completely unreasonable to me, but the other girls were appeased; they redyed their hair immediately. I bought a home hair-dye kit and colored my hair black, but that was just the start of the hell awaiting me.

My hair didn't hold color; not long after I dyed it, it would fade back to brown. Whenever that happened, the other girls tattled, and I'd be called back to the staff room and coerced into dyeing it again. My hair eventually got so damaged, and my scalp so irritated, that I had to chop off most of the hair I'd worked so hard to grow out.

My mother was so infatuated with her new partner that she paid no attention to my plight. When I told her I needed to go to a salon for a haircut, she just handed over money.

I've never forgotten the girls' smug looks when I showed up with my hair cropped. After that, I hit the books, hoping to get into a good high school that wouldn't make me change my hair if I proved it was natural. I worked hard to treat my damaged, broken hair, and slowly managed to regrow it to its old length. I taught myself makeup skills as self-defense; cosmetics were a tactic to distract from my hair.

"You'll catch cold if you sleep in a place like this, Iguchi."

I must've nodded off without realizing; a rough shake jarred me awake. Recognizing a familiar scent, I slowly opened my eyes. "Chiaki…?"

Against my expectations, Rintaro stood there. "Your face looks terrible. Were you crying?"

"No." I rubbed my eyes as I sat up, then remembered I had makeup on. The amount of eye shadow on the back of my hand was more than I'd expected to come off with just one swipe of my hand. Hurriedly taking out my compact, I confirmed that I'd completely destroyed the eye makeup I'd worked so hard on that morning. I now resembled a panda.

Everything around me looked white and cloudy—I must've still been half-asleep. I was cleaning up my messy face with makeup remover when the door rattled open.

"Hey, Rintaro, is Iguchi awake?"

It was Chiaki. His lighthearted smile must've perked me up, because all the color suddenly returned to my field of vision; the world became a bright neon that made me blink. His oil-paint scent wafted over from the seat next to mine. As my senses slowly returned, I realized I was in the art room.

"I texted you so many times, but you never answered," he told me. "I figured you were probably here. It's already time for lunch!"

He grabbed my phone from where it'd fallen on the floor and handed it back to me. Since the school festival ended, I hadn't gotten a single text, but now the screen was full of notifications thanks to Chiaki.

Whenever I skipped class, I came to the art room. It was supposed to be locked, but I knew exactly where the laissez-faire art club advisor hid the spare key.

"I told the teachers I'd make sure you attended the afternoon classes. And you can copy my notes. That'll make us square for earlier," Chiaki declared, returning an easel facing the window to its original position.

I'd fallen asleep atop a row of chairs. My joints popped and cracked as I stretched.

"You usually buy lunch at the canteen, right? Even if you go now, I think most of the good stuff will already be sold out," Chiaki added, handing me a foil-wrapped onigiri.

Rintaro looked on in surprise as Chiaki placed his lunch bag on the desk. "You brought another huge lunch."

"I'm a growing boy," Chiaki replied. "Are you buying lunch from the convenience store again, Rintaro? You can have some of mine, if you want."

Chiaki's bento box was the same size as those used by the students in sports clubs. He had enough onigiri to cover not just lunch, but breakfast *and* mid-morning and after-school snacks. They weren't a uniform shape or size, so I could tell at a glance they'd been made by a high-school boy who didn't spend much time cooking.

"Sorry about the side dishes. They're just leftovers from dinner last night," he apologized.

"Still, you put this bento together yourself, right? And first thing in the morning, to boot. That's impressive."

"Well, I'd feel bad asking Mom to do it. I go to school early for the art club."

The side dishes crammed into the bento offered a glimpse into what dinner must be like in the Sakura household. There was quite a bit of fried food, including Hokkaido-style fried chicken and fried squid tentacles, probably made with the Sakura children's palates in mind. To someone like me, who'd practically never tasted her mother's home cooking, or Rintaro, who only stocked his fridge with beer, Chiaki's bento was a treat we wouldn't trade for anything in the world.

The three of us pressed our hands together and said the customary pre-meal greeting, "Itadakimasu," then dug into the onigiri and side dishes.

"Your family sure likes sweet tamagoyaki," Rintaro noted after a bite of rolled omelet.

"My grandmother had a huge sweet tooth. She used to put sugar on everything, apparently—even tomatoes and natto."

"Sugar's surprisingly good on tomatoes, right? It almost makes them taste fruity."

These snippets of idle conversation were the best company I could've asked for. Eating lunch with Chiaki and Rintaro showed me that sharing a meal was leaps and bounds better than any solo fine-dining experience. To the three of us, the art room had become something of a secret hiding place.

Chiaki was still munching his onigiri as he tied on his apron. It was made of strong canvas material and covered with paint splotches. Removing oil paint from fabric was tough, and on top of that, he hardly ever washed the garment. Still, he wore the dirty apron all the time, which was probably why he always smelled oily.

The art club's next competition with the All Japan Senior High School Culture Federation was approaching quickly. Sports clubs participated in competitions with other high schools on specific dates, but culture clubs had to submit projects by a specific deadline, and that often involved a training or presentation component.

"Do you really have to put so much effort into this year's competition?" I asked. "You're still just a second-year."

"The national competition for art clubs will take place during the next school year. And if I win gold as a third-year, I can't submit my project to the national contest. I told you that before, remember?"

Competitions took place at district, prefectural, and national levels. Only first- and second-year student projects that earned gold at the Hokkaido Prefectural Competition could compete in the following year's national round.

"If I make it to nationals, an art school might recommend me for admission. That could make or break my future, so I've got to give it my all now."

The second year of high school was a time when many kids started thinking about what they aimed to do after graduating. Chiaki wanted to attend art school, but a lot of students failed the entrance exams straight out of high school and had to apply for another year or two before they were accepted. Chiaki probably wanted to get his hands on a recommendation for immediate admission more than anything else.

But, at the moment, I was more concerned about what was happening with my face. A deep chuckle reverberated from Rintaro's throat as he watched me eat my onigiri while fixing my makeup.

"You two may be working on different canvases, but you're both creating art," he commented.

"Hey! Don't lump me in with him!" I protested.

Chiaki just smiled, gripping a paintbrush. "You've got a point. She comes up with really outlandish makeup sometimes. I thought she'd had a fashion mishap when she came to school with that yellow stuff around her eyes."

"Yellow eye shadow was trending then! Don't you dare compare me to someone like Rintaro!"

"Hey, Rintaro's fashion sense is getting better lately. Remember when he wore those funky-colored ties back when we were first-years? Where the heck did you even buy them, Rintaro?"

"I just randomly wore ties that other people gave me. I mean, a tie's a tie, right?"

When it was just the three of us in our own little world, the atmosphere was so different from Class 2-A's. We all pretended to be something we weren't at times, but here, we could be our true selves. Rintaro, who always played a pleasant, easygoing teacher in front of everyone else, could be his actual curt self here, and Chiaki stopped acting like the epitome of an honor student.

Chiaki was working on his competition piece, a realistic landscape painting. He was painting everything in minute detail, from the rooftops to the tree branches. Oil paints, unlike watercolors, didn't dry quickly. You mixed them separately, with a solvent, and they took at least one night to dry. Each day, Chiaki diligently painted a coat, and I secretly looked forward to the moment he'd complete his masterpiece.

"I'm napping for a bit. Wake me when the warning bell rings," Rintaro said.

"That's our model teacher for you."

Since the school festival ended, Rintaro had been spending more time in the art room. The vice principal and head teacher reprimanded him sternly after Class 2-A's cross-dressing café was deemed too risqué for a high-school festival, and since Rintaro had started coming here to escape the staff room's uncomfortable atmosphere, it was hard for him to give me grief when I played hooky. He lay down on the row of chairs I'd been using and covered himself with a cloth used for sketching practice.

Chiaki got his painting ready while he finished eating his lunch. Once he was done, he crumpled the foil from the onigiri he'd eaten and got to work.

I finally finished fixing my makeup and put away my cosmetics bag, then walked to the window to let some fresh air in.

The art room's curtains were always shut so the sun wouldn't fade the paintings. I couldn't tell whether the cream-colored drapery had originally been that shade, or if it'd just yellowed slightly with age. The wind rustling through the curtains carried the sound of students hanging out in the schoolyard. Their voices mingled with Chiaki's intermittent humming and Rintaro's soft breathing.

I couldn't hear my mother flirting with her partner on the phone, screaming and crying day and night after being dumped once again, nor could I hear her taking out her anger on me whenever she got wasted.

Chiaki was so focused that he seemed not to notice me peering at him. He still smelled faintly of deodorant spray, but the scent of the art room would take over again before long.

Projects by generations of past art club members lined the walls—a world so colorful, taking it in almost hurt my eyes. Rintaro looked like an innocent baby as he slept swaddled in pure white cloth. By now, Chiaki was fully immersed in painting; his artwork was the only thing he saw. No one was around to get worked up about my hair or eyes. Only in this secret hiding place could I let my guard down fully and breathe easy.

If only these quiet moments lasted forever, I thought. Just Chiaki, Rintaro, and me, with no one to disturb us.

I used to spend a lot of time with Manabe and her friends after school, but lately I've traded karaoke microphones for art room pencils.

"I'm not *actually* in the art club, though."

"But you're always here. Just submit your intent-to-join form already."

The art room might've been quiet at lunchtime, but a few club members showed up after school. Most had glasses and wore their uniforms exactly according to the dress code—not the crowd I usually associated with. Some third-years were apparently part of the club, but none were actively participating, so Chiaki was acting as the de facto president.

"The competition's going to host a practice session on quick sketches, so I thought we'd practice a little today," he explained. "We'll set the time limit at thirty minutes."

The subject for the sketch was a plaster figurine of the iconic Venus de Milo. Everyone moved their chairs to wherever they wanted to work from; I'd secured a spot in the back of the classroom. At the sound of a buzzer, the club members started sketching away. I twirled my pencil between my fingers.

Everyone had their own way of going about the assignment. Some started with details of the figurine's face while others broadly sketched its entire outline. I noticed that the way some drew certain details betrayed their fetishes—the Venus de Milo's breasts were diminutive, but a few boys generously emphasized her chest. I also saw a couple girls enthusiastically sketching her six-pack abs.

It was raining outside, and the chilly air signaled the inevitable changing of the seasons. The weather also forced sports clubs to practice indoors. Shouts to encourage students running inside or to count out hallway strength-training exercises echoed as far as the distant corner of the building where the art room was located.

I wonder what Chiaki's doing? I mused.

Curious, I rose from my seat and glanced over. I saw him flip to a blank page in his sketchbook and start drawing. At first, I couldn't make sense of his actions; he'd draw something quickly on one page, then flip to a new one instead of adding details. He was the only one in the entire room doing anything like that, but no one else seemed to care. Terrifying intensity radiated from his back. Realizing that I couldn't bother him, I sat down again.

The buzzer eventually sounded once more, and everyone stopped drawing. No faculty members were around to critique the finished sketches since the art teacher only came on days when classes were scheduled. Instead, the club members usually showed everyone else their artwork and discussed it with each other as they pleased.

"Considering this was just your first time, Yoshino, your sketch turned out really well," Chiaki noted, peeking at one student's sketchbook.

Hearing his comment, some others gathered around to take a look. The object of their attention was Somei Yoshino, a first year who'd joined the club right before summer break. I saw her face turn bright red. Even to an amateur eye, it was obvious that her sketch of the figurine was incredibly well-balanced. I figured she must take art as her elective, so I was positively shocked to have learned that she was enrolled in the music class.

"You're so good at art, though. Why didn't you choose that as your elective?" I inquired.

"I wanted to be in my friend's class," she replied in a barely audible voice.

I wanted to ask why in the world she'd sacrificed something she was great at for such a silly reason, but I somehow held my tongue, realizing it wasn't any of my business. "If you're so easy to steamroll, then if you ever get a boyfriend, he'll dump you pretty quick."

"I don't think I'll ever have one. I don't really like men."

"What? Are you a lesbian or something?" Try as I might, I couldn't keep the snark out of my voice.

Chiaki snapped my name accusingly.

A knock at the door cut the conversation short. We could see someone peering through the door's window: Chiaki's little sister. Until recently, she'd sported a chin-length bob, but she'd come back from summer break with her hair cut short. She had Chiaki's huge eyes, and it was plain as day that they were related. She waved at us.

When Yoshino realized who it was, her face brightened immediately. "Hazuki!"

"The girls' volleyball team was doing stamina drills in the hall," Chiaki's sister told us. "Sorry we were so loud."

"Let me know when you're done. We'll head home together."

I'd heard from Chiaki that his sister joined the volleyball team when Yoshino joined the art club. They'd enrolled in such different extracurriculars that the girls' relationship was probably changing slightly already, considering sports and culture club members didn't interact much.

The volleyball team must've been taking a break, because some other players began to peer into the art room as well. "What's that funky smell?" one asked. "Is it coming from the art club?"

Hazuki gave us a quick bow, and was about to shut the door when someone strutted in. It was Manabe, and she scoffed and glowered at the students with open sketchbooks.

"Must be nice to be in the art club," she said. "You guys don't have to practice every day like us. As long as you draw a few pictures, the school foots the bill for you to attend competitions, right?"

Manabe wasn't a full member of the volleyball team. I'd heard her mention in class that they'd recruited her temporarily to support them at an upcoming tournament.

"I wish I'd joined a culture club too," she sighed. "The volleyball advisor's so annoying. I never should've agreed to this."

"Our break'll be over soon, Senpai." Hazuki practically pushed Manabe out of the classroom, although she hung back a moment to give a small nod, which the art club members returned. Some sort of quiet communication seemed to be going on between the first-years.

When only Chiaki and I were left in the art room, I asked him, "Why didn't you say something back to her?"

"Her comments didn't bother me. She's probably bottling up a lot of stress. I hear the volleyball team practices are tough."

"That still doesn't give her the right to say whatever she wants. I bet one look at your painting would've shut her up on the spot."

"In that case, though, she probably wouldn't have come back here."

"What'd be the problem with that?!" I grimaced dramatically, prompting Chiaki to smile wryly as he sharpened a pencil. "Are you not going home yet?" I added. "You aren't working on your oil painting tonight, are you?"

"I want to get a little practice in for the practical exam. I'm not that good at croquis drawing." Chiaki hoped to earn an art school recommendation by doing well at the competition, but he was also gearing up for the general entrance exam. There were prep academies for getting into art schools, and their students cranked out pieces so sophisticated that you couldn't compare them to art club projects. "If you aren't going home either, why not help me out, Iguchi?"

I went over and stood by the window, as Chiaki instructed. The rain had stopped around sunset, and the sky was partly visible through the clouds. A round, bright moon rose, and I felt the fall breeze blow through the window.

Chiaki measured perspective with a pencil, then began sketching quickly in his book. Just like when he sketched the plaster figurine, he would draw something, flip to the next page, and then repeat the process. He asked me to change my pose every five minutes, but I didn't really know what to do, so I mostly stood upright.

"How come you're rushing to finish?" I objected. "You should draw more carefully."

"Croquis drawings with a live model need to be done in a specific timeframe. This helps me practice for that. I'll actually need to draw in charcoal for the practical exam, but since I got a chance to stay late, I didn't want any time to go to waste."

The rule was that club activities had to end by six-thirty in the evening, but students could continue past then if their club advisor was still on campus. Still, most teachers had busy lives and didn't try to stick around.

"Does Rintaro always stay late?" I asked.

"Yeah. He comes in early to unlock the art room for me, too. He's supporting my art club projects *and* my post-graduation goals, so it feels like I've gotta do whatever I can to meet his expectations."

Well, that explains why Rintaro always seems so tired. As I turned my face toward the sky, the relief of solving that mystery washed over me.

"Oh! That pose is good. Don't move." Chiaki stood and turned the classroom lights off. I was looking up toward the moon, and it shone down on me like a natural spotlight.

Chiaki started drawing again, but seemed to be taking his time, in contrast with his approach to his croquis drawings earlier. Whenever I got tired and tried to lower my chin, he ordered me not to move. I leaned my head back on the windowpane, realizing for the first time just how challenging it was to stay in the same position for a long time.

"If you think the moon's pretty now, just wait until you see the harvest moon next month," he told me.

"When's that supposed to happen again? The tenth night or something?"

"Yikes. Please don't tell me you forgot that the festival for the harvest moon falls on the *fifteenth* night. I think you're mixing it up with that *Ten Nights' Dreams* book we read."

"Oh, right." I nodded. Just before summer break, we'd read some of Natsume Soseki's *Ten Nights' Dreams* in Rintaro's modern Japanese literature class.

"I had this dream. I sat with arms folded by the side of a bed where a woman lay on her back. She quietly told me she was going to die."

Those were the book's first few lines. Our textbooks only included the first chapter. More than the actual plot, what stuck in my mind was our discussion during the second half of the class.

"Natsume Soseki left us many classics, like *Kokoro* and *Botchan*," Rintaro said. "Whenever I read *Ten Nights' Dreams*, it reminds me of something that supposedly happened while Soseki was working as an English teacher."

He wrote "I love you" in English on the blackboard. It was such a common English phrase, we all knew what it meant, but no one could see why we were discussing English in a modern Japanese literature class. Still, Rintaro's tangent was a much-appreciated break from real studying.

"How would you say this in Japanese, um...Tono?"

"I love you?" Tono-kun translated when Rintaro put him on the spot.

Rintaro nodded in satisfaction. "One of Soseki's students thought the same and likewise translated this as 'I love you.' But Soseki pointed out that Japanese people don't often say 'I love you' directly. He suggested that 'The moon is beautiful, isn't it?' would be a poetic interpretation that appealed to the Japanese sensibility."

Apparently, the jury was still out on whether Soseki had actually said that. But when Rintaro glanced around his usually half-checked-out class and saw that he'd caught its interest, he tried to keep the momentum going. "Anyone know the response to Soseki's poetic 'I love you'?"

Chiaki raised his hand. "'I could just die.'"

"Correct. You're pretty familiar with Futabatei Shimei, right, Sakura?"

Chiaki was the most avid learner among Rintaro's students. As class representative, he couldn't afford to bomb his homeroom subject, so he put his nose to the grindstone studying modern Japanese literature. He'd apparently always done well in literature classes, maybe because they had a strong link to the arts.

"Rintaro wound up giving us homework on *Ten Nights' Dreams* for summer break, didn't he?" Chiaki mused.

That snapped me out of the memory. "Yeah. I had a good laugh when saw the assignment." I heard insects chirping on the breeze. The weather became brisk at the end of August, and I was a little chilly wearing only my uniform in the classroom at night.

A cloud covered the moon, and since Chiaki couldn't see what he was drawing, he paused. "About what happened earlier... I think Manabe came in here trying to find you, Iguchi."

"She went out of her way to be nasty again, you mean? What the hell?"

"That's not what I mean. I think she hoped you might agree if she complained about how annoying it was to be in a club. That you might end up skipping and hanging out with her. Maybe she was looking for a way to make peace with you."

His hypothesis blindsided me. I turned to stare at him.

He just reminded me to look upward again, then casually dropped a bomb. "She asked me out during the school festival, you know."

I somehow concealed my surprise and continued staring up.

"It was during the bonfire," he continued. "I noticed she was coming to help the scenery group a lot, so...yeah. Didn't you two have your falling out around then?"

"How'd you turn her down?"

"I told her I liked someone else, but she wouldn't stop asking if I was going out with you."

Maybe the text I'd sent wasn't the only reason things went sideways between Manabe and I. She'd had suspicions about my relationship with Chiaki, and even once she confessed her feelings and learned the truth, she'd probably steered clear of me in case interacting was awkward or hurt her self-esteem.

I sighed heavily as background details I'd been unaware of all along finally surfaced. "Love really does make people idiots."

Why did that feeling even exist? It was only a temporary illusion—one my mother was always at the mercy of. The man who was supposed to love her had ditched her and their child. All she'd done since was repeat a cycle of seeking a partner, getting hurt, lamenting her pain, and finding a new partner all over again.

The girls who'd dyed their hair in junior high weren't any better. They didn't like that the boy they were crushing on was friendly with me, and they'd lashed out in petty jealousy. Now Manabe was doing the exact same thing.

"Don't say that, Iguchi. There'll come a day when you understand how she feels."

"I don't want to understand. I don't want to be like that."

"Love isn't something willpower can stave off. Take me, for example."

I knew Chiaki had feelings for someone since we'd talked about a number of things while hanging out in the art room.

"Sometimes the sparks fly as soon as you meet someone. Sometimes you hate someone, until suddenly they're all you can think about. Sometimes you fall in love with someone you shouldn't. That's just what love is."

The clouds moved with the wind, and I saw the moon floating between them in the sky. "She called me out in front of everyone during the inspection. I doubt she wants to be friends again."

"She's just jealous of your hair. Yeah, school rules or whatever make it annoying now, but once you're an adult, it'll be great to have light-colored hair without having to dye it."

Manabe had gone to the trouble of dyeing her hair despite the school's dress code, and she'd witnessed how close Chiaki and I were to boot. From her perspective, I probably seemed to get everything I wanted. That was a total misconception, though. I didn't have anything.

"I like your hair," Chiaki added. "It looks like it's twinkling in the moonlight."

And, yes, I was in the thick of a foolish unrequited love of my own.

Chiaki's painting won gold at the district competition. There was still some time before the prefectural competition for Hokkaido, but he'd probably receive gold there too, judging from his district-level evaluation. No one from our art club had ever competed at the national level, so everybody—even the school principal—eagerly awaited the next competition.

Our school used a two-semester system, so first-semester finals fell at the end of September. They put club activities on hold during that period. Right after those exams, school went into fall break, so I didn't get many opportunities to visit the art room. With my secret hiding spot inaccessible, there was only one other place I could go.

"You need to stop coming here," Rintaro scolded me hoarsely right after waking up. "I've said it a million times already."

"I've been here since last night, and you didn't wake up once. Your sleeping face was just so cute."

"Don't tell me you plan to head straight to school from here! What if someone sees us?!"

"I'll be careful that we don't leave at the same time," I replied. "I made you breakfast, so rise and shine!"

Rintaro squinted as the morning sun shone past the blackout curtains I'd pulled open. He picked up the alarm clock he kept beside his pillow. When he saw the time, he leapt out of bed.

"Crap!" he cried, rapidly getting dressed. There was still plenty of time for him to get ready to teach, but from the way he yanked on the first shirt he spotted, I could tell he was rushing at top speed. "I'm late! The head teacher's going to have my head!"

He bit into the toast slice I'd put on the table for him, then shoved a tie he spotted on the floor into his pocket and hurried toward the door, carrying his bag and car keys.

I chased after him. "Wait! That's my tie you've got!"

"Sorry...I didn't realize." Rintaro should've recognized the tie his students wore. He saw us every day, after all. He must really have been in a hurry. He put his shoes on at the same rapid pace and rushed out with a final shout: "Make sure no one's looking when you open the door!"

I got ready myself and left his apartment. The sky was beautiful and clear, but the chilly air nipped my skin. Even doing up the last button on my blazer didn't keep the cold breeze from penetrating my blouse collar.

I had a good grasp of Rintaro's neighborhood, and I was cutting through a local park when I suddenly felt a tap on my shoulder.

"Morning, Iguchi-san." I glanced back to see Hasumi Ichika standing behind me. "I thought I saw someone who looked like you, and I was right!"

"You're alone? Where's Tono-kun?" The usual presence by her side was nowhere to be seen.

"He had to go in early for class duties," she replied, then inquired, "Do you live near here? This isn't our first time bumping into each other in this park."

"I just stayed over at my boyfriend's place last night."

"Ah, I should've guessed."

Hasumi kept walking next to me as if it were something we'd planned. She was one of the only girls who hadn't treated me differently after everything went down with Manabe.

The debate over whether or not I needed to dye my hair had eventually been swept under the rug. When we returned from fall break, Manabe ended her weeks of ignoring my existence, trying to chat with me again. We didn't go back to being friends, though. If anything, it was my turn to distance myself—her fickle attitude had put me off.

On the other hand, Hasumi-san and I had both been group leaders during the festival. We'd interacted frequently, to the point that we were now close enough to chitchat if we ran into each other.

"You're dating Tono-kun now, right?" I asked. I noticed a blush creep into her cheeks as she nodded. "You denied it so long, but it was clear that something happened."

The school festival always created a number of couples. Tono-kun and Hasumi-san were childhood friends, and they'd always been close. In fact, watching them grab at each other and play around was enough to make *me* blush. Still, I'd always gotten the sense that whatever was between them didn't include sex.

"We only made it official recently. We didn't tell anyone," Hasumi-san explained. "You're pretty sharp, Iguchi. When did you figure it out?"

"During that Japanese lit class when we got our summer homework back, I guess."

The summer homework Rintaro had assigned us was mostly a review of topics we'd covered in class, and it included a section on *Ten Nights' Dreams*. There had been a rather odd task in the mix: "Write your own response to 'The moon is beautiful, isn't it?'"

There was no correct answer to that question. We were supposed to come up with something on our own. There were already plenty of responses to choose from if you looked them up online. Rintaro had presented our responses in class, however, and he hadn't evaluated whether they were *good*. Instead, he just read them in order, starting with the response the most students had submitted.

"It was a little sad seeing how many of you said, 'I'm not ready to die,'" he muttered. "I hoped high-school students would take a little more interest in enjoying their youth." He began reading the more unique replies students had submitted; the first was mine. "'I can't see the moon.' That's quite blunt, Iguchi. I'd be pretty bummed if that was someone's response."

I'd written it like that deliberately. A few students giggled. Although no one else had submitted a point-blank rejection, it didn't seem like Rintaro had gotten many of the responses he was looking for when he gave us this assignment.

"Okay. Tono Riku. 'Because I'm looking at it with you.' You didn't seem to know much about this in class, but I can tell you put on your thinking cap over the break!" Rintaro had praised the romantic answer effusively.

I caught Tono-kun glance at Hasumi-san, trying to catch her eye, but she didn't seem to notice.

Rintaro moved to the next response. "Now we have Hasumi Ichika. 'I've always thought the moon was beautiful.'" That was the kind of response I'd expected her to write.

"You figured it out because of my response?" Hasumi-san asked as I finished explaining.

"Pretty much." It had just been the type of thing someone who'd fallen for a childhood friend would say, and no one else had written anything similar. "I had a feeling you'd always carried a torch for him."

That Japanese lit class must also have made a strong impression on Hasumi-san because we discussed it until we reached the subway station. "On that topic, whose answer did you like best, Iguchi-san?"

"I..." I started to respond, then paused to consider my answer.

There were plenty to choose from. Some students turned the tables with something like "Will you watch the moon with me forever?" Other submissions, like "The stars are more beautiful," indicated love for someone else. There were even passionate responses like "If only time could stop right now."

"I guess my favorite was 'It's beautiful because it's unattainable,'" I said finally.

"Oh, Sakura-kun's answer? That hit home, huh?"

The melody announcing the next train's arrival chimed as we headed downstairs into the station. When we spotted our train pulling into the platform, we broke into a dash so we'd make it.

As she pulled out her transit pass and cleared the entry gate, Hasumi-san continued our conversation. "I feel like some people wrote the response they thought *they'd* get if they confessed their feelings, not what they'd say if someone confessed to *them*."

As I set my own transit pass on the card reader, trying to follow her, I couldn't go through. I'd been so enraptured by our conversation that I forgot my pass didn't cover Rintaro's neighborhood station—I would have to buy a separate ticket. Hasumi-san stood waiting for me, but I urged her to go ahead.

"See you at school!" As she waved goodbye with a smile, she looked like the epitome of bliss. Being loved by the object of your affection apparently made you prettier inside and out.

Hasumi-san's comment about Chiaki's response had been unexpectedly accurate. Just like me, Chiaki was in love with someone unattainable.

The art club's Hokkaido Prefectural Competition took place shortly after fall break. Before it started, the school held a send-off event in the gym for Chiaki and the other club members. The entire student body came and listened to the principal give the art club an encouraging speech. Easels displaying various members' oil paintings were arranged onstage. They held work created in class, since the competition submissions were already en route to the venue.

The paintings varied from still lifes depicting empty bottles and apples to a portrait of a calico cat, but the one that stood out was a landscape featuring a midsummer forest. The midday trees were tinged with unfathomable color. Just looking at the piece, you felt as if cicadas might start chirping at any moment. When I first saw the painting in the art room, I'd worried about the roughness of the brushwork, but everything came into focus perfectly viewed from a distance. It was impressive just how profound an oil painting could be.

"Make sure to win us a ticket to the national championships!" the principal instructed. Chiaki just smiled at the high-pressure demand. Rintaro stood beside the stage, silently watching over his club members; beside him, the head teacher gazed at the paintings in fascination.

The send-off event was honoring other clubs as well, so once the art club's slot ended, the paintings needed to be cleared offstage. Rintaro and the art club members took the reins, but Chiaki had to hang back as he was a guest of honor. It looked like carrying some of the larger pieces would be a challenge, and so I instinctively left the row where I was sitting to lend the art club a hand.

"Thanks, Iguchi," Rintaro called as I carried off an easel. The send-off was being held first thing in the morning, so he'd been asked to come early and set up. He and the head teacher had planned to carry the paintings to the gym, which explained why he'd left his apartment in such a rush.

Once we'd put everything back, Rintaro and the art club returned to the gym. I pretended to tag along, but along the way, I turned and retraced our steps.

Having been closed overnight, the art room was stuffy with paint fumes. I opened the window to let in some fresh air and noticed Chiaki's apron lying on the floor. Someone must've bumped the easel it hung on while we tidied up.

Chiaki was already working on his next painting. The canvas side faced the window, but I casually stole a peek anyway. It was a portrait. My breath caught in my throat as I took in the image of someone gazing at the moon. The picture was still just a rough sketch, but I could immediately tell who the subject was.

What was going through his head when he sketched this? Just wondering made my chest tight. Hot tears welled in the corners of my eyes, and I tried to stave them off by burying my head in Chiaki's apron, which reeked of oil paint. That aroma wasn't enticing by any stretch of the imagination; still, it reminded me of Chiaki standing behind one of his canvases. Recalling that image overwhelmed me so much that I didn't notice someone else enter the room until they tapped my shoulder.

"Chiaki?" I said tentatively.

Rintaro peered back at me instead. "I noticed you didn't come back to the gym with us. Is everything okay? Are you crying?"

The back of the hand I'd used to wipe my eyes was covered in paint. There was probably some on my face too. Knowing I'd give myself away if I answered Rintaro, I just stared at the ground.

"The send-off's done now," Rintaro added. "You should head to class. I need to lock up this room."

I heard the footsteps of students walking through the hallways, but none seemed headed this way since we'd already tidied the art room. Rintaro took the apron from me, and when he went to hang it back on its rightful owner's easel, he also noticed the whitewashed canvas. "He started another one already? Sakura's sure passionate about his art."

Just as he was able to take a closer look at the rough sketch, I ran up behind him and threw my arms around him from behind. The impact threw Rintaro off balance, and we both fell over, bumping the easel and knocking it to the ground with a loud clatter that echoed through the room.

"What're you doing?!"

He tried to push me off, but I avoided his arms, loosening his tie to expose his neck. I'd felt his warm skin so many times before. Rintaro's familiar scent reached my nostrils; something about it was a bit like the smell of oil paint.

"Get off me, Iguchi."

I tore off my blouse, but his expression didn't change, even when I started to unhook my bra.

"Hurry up and put your clothes back on," he insisted.

"Why? Am I that unattractive?"

"Just do it. You'll catch cold like that."

"Are you gay or something, Rintaro?" I'd gone and said something rude again. *Oops.* I remembered how sharply Chiaki had barked my name when I'd said something similar not long ago.

Rintaro made the most of my temporary pause by asking, "What is it you want, Iguchi?"

"I like you, Rintaro," I replied.

"Oh, yeah?" he responded.

My perspective suddenly flipped upside down. I didn't understand what was happening at first—then I realized he'd pushed me onto the paint-smeared floor and was lying on top of me. It was the first time he'd done something like this.

"Stop it!" I screamed as he kissed me violently, his hands running over my exposed skin. I shoved him away with all my strength and managed to get out from beneath him. I clutched one of the art room's drawing sheets around myself and struggled to catch my breath as I trembled in fear.

"What is it you want?" he asked again. I couldn't say anything back. "If you need a place where you're comfortable, I can give you one. I'll keep hiding my key in the same place I always have. But what do you want from me?" He undid his rumpled tie, his tongue licking blood off his lip. It immediately turned crimson again. I must've bitten him harder than I realized. "*Who* is it you like, Iguchi?"

I could only respond by looking at the floor.

When the bell for the start of class rang, Rintaro rose to his feet. I heard the slam of the door behind him as he left, but I was still shaking like a leaf and wasn't able to raise my head. All I could do was hug myself tightly, waiting to calm down.

His words repeated in my head again and again. *"What is it you want?"*

"I..." I forced myself to speak, voice raspy, but froze in terror as I heard the art room door reopen.

"Iguchi? Are you still in here?" Chiaki's cheerful voice echoed through the room. "I gotta lock up. Let's go to class." I heard him get closer to me, one step at a time. Then he froze in his tracks as he spotted me hugging myself protectively. "Iguchi...? Rintaro told me to lock up here..." He trailed off, seemingly racking his brain for some kind of clarity. Rintaro had stormed out of the art room, leaving me behind on my own—and I was half-naked.

Despite his confusion, Chiaki was kind enough to take off his shirt and give it to me, averting his gaze so I could cover myself. "I see. So...*that's* how it was between you guys." He laughed dryly and sat on the floor, glancing at the fallen easel. "Yeah...I knew you met up here a lot. It's okay. I won't tell anyone."

"We haven't been..."

"You don't need to lie. I figured something like this would happen at some point."

"You've got it all wrong."

Rintaro's blood was still on my lips. I wiped it off, but the sensation lingered there. I'd finally gotten what I hoped for, but it left me with an overwhelming sense of self-loathing. As I bit my own lip, it was like the floodgates of my heart burst wide open. Keeping my gaze locked on the floor, I confessed my feelings with the last bit of strength I could muster. "I'm sorry, Chiaki. I wound up falling for you."

He glanced once more at the toppled easel, and relief seemed to ripple over him. It was still just a rough outline with no color at all. Soon, he'd cover it with several coats of paint that would conceal the drawing beneath, like it'd never existed at all. That's why he'd chosen to draw Rintaro on the canvas.

"And after you opened up to me, too," I said. "I'm so sorry."

Chiaki and I had spent hours together in the art room. We'd talked about lots of silly things, occasionally whispering about matters of the heart. He'd told me his feelings for Rintaro, which proved how much he trusted me.

Chiaki knew those feelings would be fruitless. He'd experienced painful love many times through his childhood, and he'd made up his mind never again to fall for someone—but his heart had other ideas when he met Rintaro.

I still couldn't forget the expression on Chiaki's face when he opened his heart and revealed everything to me. He could never tell Rintaro how he felt, but I'd taken it upon myself to keep a watchful eye on his unwavering devotion from the sidelines. Chiaki was someone who appreciated subtle romantic gestures and knew roundabout ways to express love, like saying the moon looked beautiful.

I had nothing but respect for him. In fact, I envied his pure-hearted ability to love. Before long, my own feelings had turned romantic, and I was the one who'd betrayed our friendship.

"I'm sorry," I repeated.

Chiaki sat on the floor, seemingly lost for words. I could tell he didn't know whether to cry, laugh, or get mad. As he mulled over how to express his feelings, I reached out to stroke his cheek.

"Rintaro's here," I said, cupping his cheeks in both hands. When he looked up in stunned surprise, I kissed him on the lips. Part of me wanted to claim just a fraction of his feelings by any means. Chiaki himself could never touch the object of his affection, but I'd thought maybe I could do it instead, and he could feel Rintaro's lips and warm skin through me. I loved Chiaki so much I was willing to become an utter fool in the process.

I'd never wanted to be under love's thumb. I didn't want relationships like my mother's—ultimately, she was always cast aside. And I didn't want to find myself eternally seeking impossible love. That was just what I ended up doing, though. I wanted Chiaki's pure love for myself, even if only the tiniest spoonful.

Chiaki's eyes scanned the floor for the fallen canvas as I tried desperately to distract him with my kisses. Once he completed the painting, Rintaro's face would be gone. It had been me moongazing that night, so in the end, the finished product would probably depict my face. That was how Chiaki would keep protecting his heart.

But I wanted his feelings for myself so badly, I didn't care if it was fake love. "Chiaki..."

The two of us were so lost in thought, we didn't hear the sound of footsteps approaching. It was too late for us to pull apart by the time the door flew open.

"What do you think you're doing?!" a voice bellowed as our secret hiding place was desecrated.

The head teacher had opened the art room door and caught Chiaki and me in the act.

He was a P.E. teacher who mostly focused on his role as volleyball advisor. Apparently, he'd wanted to see the art room after hearing about it from some members of the girls' volleyball team. Usually, no one dropped by the art room, but Chiaki and I had made a major blunder assuming that would always be the case.

We'd hoped to go to class, but instead, the head teacher took us straight to the student guidance room. Chiaki and I sat side-by-side on the ancient sofa, and the head teacher glared at us with an intensity that made our hair and uniform inspection seem like a walk in the park.

"We may need to contact your parents," he told us, "But I'd like to hear what you two have to say first." He leaned forward, sitting with his arms crossed and legs wide apart. Although he seemed to be maintaining his cool somehow, he'd clearly been incredibly agitated since discovering us in the art room.

"First of all, are either of you hurt anywhere?" asked Rintaro, who'd also joined the meeting as our homeroom teacher and the art club advisor. Despite making a show of asking about his pupils' physical safety, he sat in an easy chair, obviously trying to distance himself. His lip wound had stopped bleeding and scabbed over.

"Was this consensual?" the head teacher asked.

Neither of us attempted to answer, and awkward silence filled the room. No force had been involved in what Chiaki and I had done In that regard, they'd probably consider the act consensual. If we confirmed that, though, we'd basically be saying we were dating.

"We're aware that Sakura's big competition is coming up. We don't want to have to make a stir over this. Depending on what you say, though, we may have to handle this as a case of sexual misconduct."

After a moment's hesitation, Chiaki broke the silence first. "It was consensual."

"No! I forced him!" I didn't miss a beat contradicting his claim. Chiaki's eyes widened in surprise. He looked like he was going to say something else, but I continued before he could get another word in. "We were just fooling around. We didn't go all the way. I don't remember seeing 'cuddling on school grounds' forbidden anywhere in the school code."

"That sort of conduct is completely inappropriate at school."

"So you're saying it'd be okay at a hotel? Or one of our houses?"

Many students became sexually active after starting high school. I was sure plenty of couples went all the way on school grounds and just hadn't been caught by teachers yet.

I kept arguing with the head teacher, not giving Chiaki a single chance to cut in. All Rintaro could do was watch the exchange in silence. His gaze made me uncomfortable, and I shook my head like I was trying to cast it off.

"As teachers, we want students to have a solid, wholesome high school experience," the head teacher insisted. "What I witnessed today can't just be shrugged off with a smile."

"How come everything has to be so restricted at school?" I demanded. "The only reason any of us are here is because our parents had sex!"

"What I'm saying is that you're still *children*."

If I'd backed Chiaki—pretended the encounter was consensual, told them Chiaki and I were a couple—this probably wouldn't have turned into such a big deal. They likely would've let us off with a scolding about acting properly at school. But I didn't want that lie to hurt Chiaki.

"School's a place where you learn to follow rules," the head teacher insisted. "The ability to follow the school code will be an advantage when you finally join society as an adult."

"If that were true, you'd make me change my natural hair color too." Not budging an inch, I opened a can of worms—our battle during the hair and uniform inspection.

The head teacher went quiet, then said, "Iguchi, you and Sakura aren't a couple, are you? If not, I don't think a physical relationship is appropriate. On top of the argument that you should only be intimate with someone you *love*, I know you're aware that there are health risks involved as well."

I was silenced by his sound logic. He wasn't being at all condescending; as P.E. teacher, he was responsible for teaching our health class.

"I have my own children," he added. "I know they'll grow up someday, and I'd rather they have that type of relationship with someone they truly love. That hope extends to my students as well."

It didn't seem like he'd let this incident go with a slap on the wrist. I should've lied right away—bringing up all that other stuff just poured fuel on the fire. *What do I say now, though? How do I convince him to let us off the hook?*

"Maybe there's something about this situation that you're uncomfortable discussing with teachers?"

The head teacher was already a step ahead of me. He apparently thought that, if pushing wouldn't work, pulling might. His change in tactics was so sudden that the wind went out of my sails, and a prolonged silence permeated the student guidance room.

"Sir, I—" Chiaki started hesitantly.

Then Rintaro—who'd barely made his presence known this entire time—cut him off. "When did you paint that forest, Sakura?"

"As a first-year," Chiaki replied.

Rintaro shook his head, as if that wasn't the answer he'd been looking for. "What *season* did you paint it, I mean?" he clarified.

It took the rest of us some time to understand what he meant. "Summer," Chiaki eventually responded, still seeming perplexed. His big eyes were wider than usual with surprise. "The middle of summer, to be specific. When cicadas were chirping in the forest."

"Summer, huh?" Rintaro murmured to himself as if pondering something.

The head teacher couldn't hide his confusion. "Kakei-sensei?"

"All this time, I haven't known whether that painting captured summer, fall, or even spring," Rintaro continued. "I did everything I could not to show it, but I couldn't tell what color the trees were."

His confession immediately reminded me of his apartment's décor. It was full of dark colors—coffee-colored sheets, navy curtains. And he always wore ties in similar shades. Maybe that wasn't because he was lazy, but because he couldn't confidently choose anything else. That would explain why he'd accidentally picked my tie up that morning—he couldn't tell what color it was. And apparently, everything in Chiaki's painting—from the leaves to the tree trunks—had looked the same shade of brown to him.

"Still, I managed to become a teacher," Rintaro added. "And although I can't tell what color a stoplight is, I could see the light's position, so I got my driver's license. You never had any idea, did you?"

I'd spent plenty of time with Rintaro and never noticed so much as a hint of color blindness. The head teacher's surprised expression told me this was the first he'd heard of it as well, so even Rintaro's coworkers must've been completely in the dark.

"As a child, I loved drawing," Rintaro told us. "I'd use crayons to cover my entire paper. But one day, my friend asked why I drew all the trees completely brown."

Rintaro couldn't have understood my insecurity over my hair. To him, slightly different hair colors must've looked identical. Still, he'd tried to understand my concern in his own way and create a comfortable space for me.

"Everyone has a secret or two," he continued. "Even if you're looking at the same thing, you might see something a different way from someone else. I don't think either of you need to force yourselves to conform, and you don't need to tell us everything about what happened if you're not comfortable with that."

As Chiaki and I stayed silent, Rintaro added, "Keeping a secret all to yourself can be surprisingly painful, though. If it's too much to handle on your own, you can rely on me—or anyone else you trust. It's okay to vent your emotions to adults like us before those emotions hurt you. That's one of your privileges as kids."

Rintaro had realized my feelings for him were a lie long ago. He was faking something himself, so he was sensitive to others' dishonesty. He could never mistake superficial whispers or reluctant efforts to seduce him for true love.

He turned to the head teacher. "Under the circumstances, what would you say to putting this incident aside, sir? I don't want to *force* these kids to reveal any more of their secrets to us than they have." Apparently, Rintaro also knew how to forgive lies. "You were modeling for Sakura's painting, right, Iguchi? I think you might've taken it too far. Don't you agree...?"

He was so insistent, all Chiaki and I could do was nod in agreement.

"But Kakei-sensei..." said the head teacher.

"We just need to wait for the day when they're comfortable enough to tell us. That's fine. As their homeroom teacher, I know these two well enough to recognize that they didn't act thoughtlessly." He followed up by offering to treat the head teacher to a drink sometime, which seemed to finally coax him into conceding.

Rintaro was completely playing into the reputation he'd built himself at school. Perhaps Chiaki and I—who knew his true nature—held a special place in his heart.

The painting Chiaki entered in the Hokkaido Prefectural Competition didn't win him a ticket to the national round. But as soon as the competition ended, the third-years retired from the art club, and Chiaki was elected the new club president. He'd already acted the part so long that he had no problem advising underclassmen on their projects. When he wasn't taking part in club activities, he worked on his new painting.

Rintaro managed the art room key strictly now, and if any student needed to enter the room afterhours, he was present. That was one of the compromises he'd made to ease the head teacher's many complaints and ensure no similar incidents would ever occur in the art room again. Still, Chiaki, Rintaro, and I continued to use that room as our secret hiding place.

"Just join the art club officially already, Iguchi. Having an extracurricular on your report card makes a difference during college entrance exams, you know," Chiaki said.

"No, thanks. I suck at drawing pictures."

"The art club isn't about just drawing, though."

Despite everything that had happened, the three of us still spent time together. The only difference was that I couldn't get into Rintaro's apartment anymore. He probably hid the spare key somewhere else.

The days shortened as fall progressed, and the moon came out earlier. I used that as a reason to spend time with Chiaki by modeling for his new painting. I was the only one who knew what he'd actually drawn in his rough draft. The figure currently adorning the canvas had long hair that fluttered in the breeze. I sometimes worried about whether the painting's current iteration satisfied Chiaki, but he kept working on it with no hesitation whatsoever.

We turned off the classroom lights, and Rintaro ended up dozing off. I spoke in a hushed voice so I wouldn't wake him. "You two stayed in the same hotel room, right? Are you sure nothing happened?"

"Stop asking me that, Iguchi. We may have shared a room, but we still had our own beds. Rintaro just drank a beer and fell asleep right away."

Sounds like he sticks to his routine even on business trips, I thought.

"Well, I did consider giving him a kiss or two if the opportunity presented itself," Chiaki added. "But that urge passed when I saw his sleeping face."

Faint moonlight currently bathed that same peaceful countenance. It looked almost like a baby's.

"Starting next year, after school, I'll attend art prep classes," Chiaki went on. "So I can relax and draw something I like for the next competition."

"If you ever need me to strip for you, just say the word."

"I've seen enough of that to last a lifetime, thanks."

He expertly applied some hues he'd blended on his palette to his canvas. He was working on the moongazing figure's hair. It picked up the silver moonlight and brightened toward the tips of the strands where it almost twinkled.

"Who's the model for your painting?" I asked.

"You, obviously. Why are you even asking?"

"Well, I know that you know I'm bustier than that."

The figure in the painting was completely nude, but it didn't have breasts or male genitalia. Maybe Chiaki planned to paint garments eventually. He seemed to be mulling over how to proceed as he went along.

"It's fine as it is right now. Like I said, I decided to draw things the way I want to," he replied. He was gazing directly at the painting with such intensity that I found myself envying the moongazing figure, despite being its model.

"Oh," Chiaki added. "I did decide on this piece's title, though."

"You did?"

"I've had it in mind since the moment inspiration struck. I'm sure even Rintaro won't be confused about what's going on in this painting." Unlike the trees, which changed with each season, the moon remained stationary in the sky year-round. It was always in the same place, whether it was night or midday.

"So? What's it called?" I asked.

Chiaki sighed and smiled softly. "The moon is beautiful, isn't it?"

I wondered whether that was literally the title, or if Chiaki meant something else. Either way, although part of me still wanted to believe Chiaki might just have aimed those words at me, he hadn't. They were a confession of love to the painting's real model. I looked up at the sky, swallowing the tears that threatened to spill from my eyes. The moon floating above me was so round, it looked like someone had poked a hole in the night sky.

"The moon is beautiful, isn't it?" I repeated.

"It's beautiful because it's unattainable," Chiaki murmured softly.

I kept gazing at the far-off moon, savoring the tenderness of those words.

PART 4

The Hidden Calico

Riku Can't Be a Goddess

WE FOUND OURSELVES clasping hands as the first notes of "Turkey In The Straw" played. It was a folk song in which boys and girls paired up and danced together. Glancing down at the schoolyard below, I noticed the students who'd been raucously dancing the jenkka were scattering to the sidelines. Only couples stood around the bonfire now. Some looked clumsy and unsure while others appeared very comfortable holding hands, perfectly in sync.

Although we danced along too, our rhythm was off. We'd practiced the folk dances in P.E., but the linoleum classroom floor didn't provide much traction while doing the steps in bare feet.

When I stepped on her foot, we stopped dancing. "Sorry."

After she lost her balance and I caught her, we were practically face-to-face. We hadn't exchanged many words as we watched the post-festival celebration from our classroom. Just the slight warmth we felt radiating from each other's bodies satisfied us as we stood side by side.

I was about to step back again, but her hands cupped both my cheeks. The fragrance she'd dabbed on her wrists was unisex, but always seemed to smell sweeter on her. I placed my hands over hers; they were so small that my palms fully covered them.

Her cheeks reflected the bonfire, glowing crimson, and—although she didn't apply makeup often—on this special occasion, she wore the gloss I'd given her. I felt drawn to her glistening lips. I'd kissed them countless times, but however hard I wished it, they couldn't belong to me. I didn't possess her small hands or soft lips, nor the sweet scent of her skin.

Yet she still called me beautiful. "You look gorgeous, Riku."

The costume group had sewn me a white cocktail dress to wear at the school festival. Even though it was made of cheap sateen, it had looked almost like silk in the cross-dressing café's dim lighting. Its design was simple, but its well-planned draping emphasized the womanly curves I lacked.

The moment I laid eyes on the garment, my heart leapt with joy, but I just couldn't go through with wearing it. I was well aware that the costume group had pulled all-nighters creating our outfits, but I spent the entire festival wearing a black suit. I could only bring myself to try on the white dress at Ichika's urging when we found ourselves alone in the classroom during the post-festival celebration.

"Ichika," I whispered.

Ichika stood on tiptoe to kiss me, and I leaned down to meet her halfway. *When did the height difference between the two of us get so big?*

She always trembled the moment we started kissing. Feeling the slight quiver in her lips made me want to throw my arms around her and squeeze as hard as I could. I controlled that urge, placing my hands on her shoulders instead.

To be frank, I was terrified of breaking her. Her porcelain skin looked like it would tear if my nails scratched it. Her neck was so slender, it wouldn't take much force to snap. Her back was so slight, I'd probably stifle her if I hugged her too tightly. She was dainty and delicate—my very own treasure.

"Riku...?" She looked so innocent as she gazed up at me.

Pulling her close, I kissed her aggressively, pushing my tongue between her lips and into her mouth. She was startled at first, and tried to pull back, but my hand held the nape of her neck. It was so slender, I was once again struck by how easy it would be to break.

However pretty the dress I wore, however long my wig, however delicately I applied my makeup—I couldn't hold a candle to what Ichika naturally had. I felt tempted to smother her in my embrace, to leave deep scratch marks on her skin. If I gobbled down every part of her, head to toe, could I possibly be like her? I was incredibly envious.

"Riku, what's wrong? Are you crying?"

Ichika gazed up at me with a worried expression after our mouths parted. I'd sucked her lips so hard that they looked swollen and painful.

She was always concerned about me; hearing it made my heart ache. I closed my eyes to keep the tears from spilling, but a single droplet escaped. Ichika's slender finger wiped it away. Despite my aggression, she wrapped me in an embrace and gently patted my back, like she was consoling a child. I buried my face in the nape of her neck, filling my lungs with her sweet fragrance. She whispered again and again that everything was going to be okay, using the same big-sisterly tone I'd heard countless times since we were children.

No matter what, I could never be her.

The melody of a folk dance floated through the open window, repeating again and again. No one would come back into the classroom until the song was over. Yet before long, this moment—my last time ever wearing a skirt—would end.

When fall break ended and second semester began, we'd reached the midpoint of our three years of high school. First semester had revolved around prepping for the school festival, but this semester would see us take our school trip—the pinnacle of our high school lives. Our class was almost buoyant at the prospect of traveling to Honshu, which we rarely had the chance to visit. As if to burst our collective bubble, though, we'd also received a form on which to write our post-graduation plans. The time to seriously consider what we'd like to do after high school was finally here.

As I gazed absently out the classroom window into the schoolyard, Sakura Chiaki tapped my shoulder. "Where's your sweetheart, Riku? It's weird seeing you here this late. Did you fight?"

I didn't belong to any school clubs, so I usually went home right after class let out. I could probably count the times I'd been in a classroom after school on one hand. The sound of sports clubs practicing on the field was unfamiliar to me. I could hear the school orchestra playing a tune in the music room too. The school atmosphere underwent refreshing changes outside class time.

"No," I replied. "She has her parent-teacher-student conference today. I'm waiting until she's done."

We were supposed to review that form with our post-graduation plans at the parent-teacher-student conference. There was only time to schedule a few each day, so it was taking a while to get through them all. Mine had been held relatively early, but Ichika's ended up being toward the end, since her family had trouble finding a day when they could come in.

"Ah, right. Today was Hasumi-san's turn, huh?" said Chiaki. "So, you're waiting for her? You two are as lovey-dovey as always."

I responded to his teasing with a generous smile. Ichika and I had only gotten together recently, but we were childhood friends who'd spent practically every moment with each other, so everyone believed we'd been a couple forever.

"I hope her conference goes well," Chiaki added. "My parents and I ended up fighting in front of Rintaro. I still can't forget how awkward he looked."

Our homeroom teacher, Kakei Rintaro, had told us to discuss our plans with our families ahead of the conferences. It seemed that, every year, at least a few parents didn't see eye to eye with their children and squabbled during their conference, leaving the homeroom teacher to do damage control. Fortunately, my conference came and went without a hint of trouble.

"I thought you were set on going to art school, Chiaki. Why would you fight with your parents?"

"I told them that, if I can't get in right after high school, I want to spend the year working a job before reapplying," Chiaki sat in the chair in front of me with an exasperated look that seemed to say "Duh."

"I hear it's tough getting into art school right after graduation."

"Yeah. It's basically a given that you need to prep an extra year or two before they'll accept you. I tried to earn a recommendation by making the national competition, but I guess that was too much for someone as minor as me to ask."

I hadn't seen Chiaki's submission to the Hokkaido Prefectural Competition, but I'd heard it was good enough to win gold, so I knew he was pretty talented artistically.

"I have a little sister, so I don't want to burden my parents," Chiaki continued. "Instead of going to some middle-of-the-road vocational school, I figured I'd hit the ground running by holding down a job while I try to get into a real art school."

"I'm jealous. You know exactly what you want to do," I muttered, not intended the words to slip out.

Chiaki's big eyes grew even larger. "I thought you were going to college. Which school's your first choice?"

On my form, I'd listed a few four-year colleges that were almost sure shots, given my grades. My top three included both public and private schools; Chiaki let out a low whistle when I listed them.

"You've always gotten good grades," he pointed out. "You probably could've enrolled at an even better high school than this one. Why'd you apply here?"

"I thought the girl's uniform was cute."

"That's a stupid reason."

"Like you're one to talk." An arts-focused boarding high school had apparently scouted Chiaki during junior high. I'd been surprised to hear that he turned down their invitation because he wanted to attend school near his house.

"What's Hasumi-san want to do?" Chiaki asked.

"All she's said is that she doesn't know yet. I'm sure she'll end up going to college, though."

"In that case, why don't you both try to get into the same one?" he suggested casually.

"It's not a high school application, you know. We shouldn't base our futures off something like enrolling with a partner." I glared at Chiaki.

He didn't seem at all intimidated. Resting his cheek on his palm, he gazed into the schoolyard. "Really? Attending with the person I love would be a good enough reason for me to apply somewhere. Watching you and Hasumi-san, getting to be with that person almost looks like a miracle."

I'd made friends with Chiaki soon after starting high school, but even as a second-year, he didn't seem close to getting a girlfriend. I'd seen him hang out with Iguchi a few times, but he always insisted they were just friends.

"You and Hasumi-san are next-door neighbors in the same apartment complex, right? You went to the same preschool, elementary, junior high, and even high school—don't you want to be with her in the future too?"

"Well, yeah."

Having Ichika by my side felt like a given. I couldn't imagine a day when she wouldn't be there. *If didn't have her in my life, what would I be doing right now?*

In junior high, the boys' uniform had a tie and the girls' had a ribbon. The ribbon was on an adjustable strap, so the girls could style their ribbons casually. That wasn't possible with the ties, though; they were simple clip-ons that attached to our collars. I often left mine at home on purpose.

When choosing which high school entrance exams to take, my first choice was a school without a uniform, but I was called to the teacher's office and was convinced to shoot for a better school. The elite schools offered either a traditional gakuran or a blazer-and-trousers combination as the boys' uniform, but all the girls' uniforms had a blazer-style top.

I was going to Ichika's room every day at that point. I'd moved my painstakingly-acquired cosmetics collection over there, and I spent my time using the products to make Ichika over with makeup looks I'd learned by watching others. It was so much fun fishing through her closet and dressing her up like my personal doll.

At first, I usually did that dressed as a boy. I was content just being surrounded by cute, girly items. Ichika and I lived in the same apartment complex, in units with the same layout—we basically even had the same room. Most of the things in her room were mine, but the fact that she was holding on to them made their elegance and sophistication skyrocket.

"Is it true you decided not to attend high school, Riku?" she'd asked. "Will you tell me why?"

The reason was that I'd felt so pressured to pick a school that I'd exploded, declaring that I wasn't going at all. I offered Ichika no response, however, squeezing a teddy bear and stubbornly refusing to talk. I'd already dressed Ichika up, but in contrast, I still wore my school uniform.

"I'd love it if we could attend the same high school," she continued. The tension building inside me dissipated a little when I learned we were on the same page about that.

"I don't want to wear a tie," I admitted.

Boys wouldn't be allowed to wear ribbons. After how hard it had been to deal with that discrepancy in junior high, I wasn't confident I could put up with it in high school.

"You don't want to wear a tie?" she repeated.

"I want to wear the same uniform you will, Ichika." It took a lot of courage to admit how I felt to her.

Ichika, however, responded with a completely nonchalant suggestion. "Well, what if *I* wear a tie too? We can't wear the same ribbon, but boys *and* girls wear ties at plenty of schools. I've actually always thought it would be cool to wear a uniform that had one."

She excitedly flipped through a magazine about high school entrance examinations. It just so happened to have a special feature on uniforms at high schools in our city; Ichika kept gushing over how cute and stylish they were, as if browsing a teen fashion collection.

I watched her in silence. There *were* a number of schools where all the uniforms included ties, but attending one would stick me with the same uniform style I'd worn in junior high for the next three years. There were bound to be plenty of days when I'd get in trouble for "forgetting" my tie at home.

I glared at the magazine so intensely, I thought I might burn a hole through it. I didn't even notice Ichika slip something around my neck. Before I could ask what she was doing, I heard a soft click as she clipped her ribbon on me.

"Wow! That looks great on you, Riku!" she squealed. "When we graduate, I'll give it to you. You can put it on in my room whenever you feel like it. You can wear anything you want here."

"Ichika..."

She was doing her best to cheer me up, but I could tell she was nervous. Seeing her slightly awkward smile helped make up my mind—I would attend whichever school Ichika went to.

And now, here we were, second-years at the same high school.

"Actually, Rintaro gave me a lot of good advice," Ichika told me.

She'd come over after finishing her parent-teacher-student conference. Her mother walked us home, but all Ichika had to say was, "I'm heading to Riku's room for a bit," and permission was granted. That was one of the perks of being a family friend.

I held Ichika from behind as she sat on my bed, fishing through her bag for something. As I stroked her thighs under her skirt, she pinched me sharply.

"Come on," she whined. "Listen to me."

She pulled a bunch of pamphlets out of her bag. She hadn't made plans for after graduation, so Rintaro had supplied tons of options—information and brochures on vocational schools, colleges, and even opportunities for studying abroad. The documents demonstrated his desire to see his students reach their highest potential. I flipped through them, then suddenly paused.

"That place is holding an info session next week. Want to go together?" Ichika asked.

We were peering at a pamphlet for a beauty school. It seemed to teach a comprehensive selection of subjects including hairstyling, nail artistry, fashion, and even modeling. It also had a sister school focused on fashion design; apparently, some beauty school graduates enrolled there afterward to further their studies. I'd been aware of the school, but I hadn't mentioned it on the form outlining my post-graduation plans.

"You really want to go somewhere like this, don't you?" asked Ichika.

I *was* very interested in working as a hairstylist or makeup artist. I should've known that Ichika—the person closest to me all these years—would have a read on my true feelings.

I normally portrayed myself as a high school boy with no particular interest in beauty. Only Ichika knew I often wore women's clothing after school, studied makeup tutorial videos daily, and even memorized every product of various companies' makeup lines. That was why I couldn't bring up a career in the beauty industry at my parent-teacher-student conference.

"How about we check out a few beauty schools together?" Ichika suggested. "If you come with me, it shouldn't be a problem. No one will blink if you say you tagged along with your girlfriend."

"Everyone will think *you* want to attend beauty school if we do that."

"That's okay. I still haven't decided what I want to do. Besides, watching you *has* inspired me to wear more stylish clothes and get better at my hair and makeup."

My arms squeezed Ichika involuntarily. I felt like a glimmer of hope was suddenly shining down on my murky future plans. If she and I attended beauty school together, I could openly develop my hair and makeup expertise. Male beauticians weren't uncommon, and studying esthetics would probably be way more practical than attending four years of university just because it felt like the thing to do.

I planted a kiss on Ichika's lips, and she earnestly reciprocated. When we finally pulled back from each other, she was smiling bashfully. It was so adorable that I couldn't help hugging her even tighter. Ichika always had so much respect for me—I was sure we'd be inseparable from now on.

When Iguchi Hikaru spotted me at the beauty school info session, she couldn't hide her surprise. "You're here solo, Tono-kun? Where's Hasumi-san? I was looking forward to walking around with her."

Plenty of students had attended the info session in their uniforms, but Iguchi wore her own clothes head to toe. She'd tied her hair up in a soft dumpling-style bun that exposed the nape of her slender neck. It was kind of cool to see her sport a different look than usual.

"Ichika came down with a fever this morning," I explained.

"Oh. That's too bad. Seems like a cold's going around recently."

Iguchi was part of our class's in-crowd, but she and Ichika appeared to be getting close lately.

Each passing day got colder, and the changing of the seasons seemed to make it easier to fall ill. Ichika and I had been naked the previous night, so maybe she'd had gotten a chill. She tried to attend the info session with me, but she was dazed with fever. I made her rest and headed out on the subway on my own.

"You were just going to tag along with Hasumi-san, weren't you? Why'd you come all the way out here by yourself?"

There was no way I could spill the truth, that I honestly hadn't planned to come after Ichika got sick, but she'd basically forced me out the door. "This is the school Ichika was most hopeful about," I told Iguchi. "I said I'd check it out and tell her about it later."

"Of course you did. Must be nice having such a committed boyfriend."

After registering, Iguchi and I opened the campus map, looked inside, and somehow I ended up touring the premises together. I was secretly grateful to have someone else there as I'd been a little anxious about doing this alone.

"Which course was Hasumi-san most interested in?"

"The...hair and makeup one, I guess?"

"Why don't we check that out first, then?"

Each department was holding its own trial events. Some popular ones—like the event run by the nail artistry department—were full, so we'd need to wait until the next time slot opened.

"Is there anything you want to see, Iguchi?"

"I'm interested in that hair and makeup course as well. And the sister school focused on fashion design will have an info session next week—I'm thinking about going there too."

Iguchi was a perfectionist when it came to appearance, and she'd created the flattering dresses the boys wore at the cross-dressing café. A career in fashion design seemed right up her alley; she'd probably been born to work as some kind of style professional.

When we opened the door to the hair and makeup department, the first thing we saw was a row of mannequin heads. To tell the truth, it was a bit unsettling to see so many heads with the same features and hairstyle lined up next to each other, but the sight would probably be mundane to any student attending this school.

An instructor was running the info session, with current students acting as assistants. They split the guests into small group and Iguchi and I wound up in the same one.

"Welcome to the hair and makeup info session," the instructor began. "We want you to see what an actual class in this department is like, so some first-year students will teach you to cut hair on a mannequin. Don't let them phone it in—if you enroll here, you'll be taking part in this kind of activity!"

That speech certainly placed pressure on the students. Some laughed wryly, but the atmosphere didn't seem negative. Most of the first-years were still in their late teens, much closer in age to me and Iguchi than their teachers.

"I'm in charge of this group," one told us. She was very tall, with long hair that accentuated her height. "I'm Miyake, but you can call me Mike."

Several assistants were helping each group, and "Mike" would apparently lead ours. She began by explaining how to hold the scissors. This lesson was technically on cutting hair, but few attendees even knew how to section it adequately. Mike-san ended up arranging most of the mannequins' hair before demonstrating how to cut it. Still, watching her do so was a valuable experience for all us observers.

Most of the group members got flustered attempting to cut the mannequins' hair. When Mike-san passed me the scissors, I tried to imitate haircuts I'd seen before. I had plenty of experience playing with Ichika's hair, but now I was so nervous that my palms were clammy.

When Mike-san noticed I was holding my breath, she tried to get me to relax. "You're Tono-kun, right? Where do you go to high school again?" She gazed at me with a big-sisterly expression, her long hair swaying around the small of her back.

I told her the name of the high school Iguchi and I attended.

Mike-san practically howled with delight. "That's the school that held the cross-dressing café, right?"

"You knew about that?"

"That café caught our attention. There are alumni from your high school enrolled here, after all. You outdid yourselves!"

"I'm…happy to hear that." Iguchi's face reddened at Mike-san's high praise.

Seeing Iguchi's reaction, Mike-san widened her catlike eyes in surprise. "Wait. Don't tell me that was *your* class's café?"

When we confirmed it was, even our group's other assistants reacted. They listened to us chat with Mike-san as they instructed the other visitors.

"Who was in charge of hair and makeup?" Mike-san asked.

"Th-that was…me," Iguchi stuttered.

It was Iguchi's turn to cut hair now, but Mike-san seemed more interested in discussing the cross-dressing café than demonstrating what to do. "Did you make the outfits from scratch? Designing clothes for the male figure is pretty challenging, huh?"

"Yeah… That's what got me interested in fashion design."

"That school next door is really good as well. We hold a joint festival with them, and students from both schools stage a fashion show together. If you're interested, I highly recommend checking them out."

Iguchi gripped the scissors, shoulders tense. Her previously perfect dumpling-style bun was loosening. She'd arranged her hair by pulling out and feathering some of the ends for volume, but the style was starting to look untidy.

Mike-san seemed to have noticed. "Your hair's coming undone. Want me to fix it?"

"Yes, please, if it's okay."

After Iguchi's turn ended, Mike-san had her sit in a chair. She removed the bobby pins holding the bun in place, returning the style to the ponytail Iguchi had started from. "Your hair's beautiful," Mike-san remarked. "Did you just dye it?"

"This is my natural color."

"Really?! What a lovely shade! I'm so jealous."

Iguchi's face twisted into an expression I'd never seen her make before at the compliment. "I've been told I need to dye it black so many times."

"People might tell you that while you're still in high school, but once you're an adult, everyone will be so envious. Colored hair eventually ends up damaged—enjoying that shade without dyeing it is such a luxury."

I noticed Iguchi repeatedly clench and relax her jaw as Mike-san talked. At first, I wondered why she was acting so awkwardly. Then I realized she wasn't used to having her hair praised.

"Everyone goes nuts dyeing their hair once they start classes here," Mike-san continued. "You should keep yours as-is, though. It's a trait that makes you unique, so you should cherish it."

I remembered that Iguchi got some grief during the hair and uniform inspection after summer break. Still, I'd never realized she was so self-conscious about her hair color. She never let that show at school.

When she was done cooing over Iguchi's hair, Mike-san finally got back on track. She pulled Iguchi's hair elastic out.

"Most people gather their hair loosely if they want a messy bun, but it's better to wrap it tightly around the base to start."

She separated Iguchi's hair into two sections, intertwining them like she was making donut twists. Then she wove the twisted hair tightly around the elastic at the base of the bun, ensuring there were no gaps at all. That inevitably made the bun appear smaller, like the hairstyle ancient warriors were often depicted with.

At some point, the instructor had come over and stood watching Mike-san's work, but Mike-san was so caught up in styling Iguchi's hair that she didn't notice the audience forming.

"You should slide the bobby pins in perpendicular to the scalp," she continued. "Lift the bun and fasten them directly to the elastic at the base...just like this. See? Even with only two bobby pins, it won't lose its shape."

The unused bobby pins sat on the table. I'd practiced similar styles on Ichika, but I'd always relied on lots of pins to pull them off. Iguchi seemed impressed too; I heard her murmur "That's amazing!" under her breath.

"If the base is stable, the bun won't fall apart, even if you pull hair out for texture. Try it yourself next time," Mike-san added, teasing the bun to give it volume. The finished style was much more stable than the bun Iguchi had made herself.

Some other assistants who'd also finished their teaching duties had joined the instructor to watch Mike-san. When she realized how many eyes were on her, she let out an exaggerated squeal of surprise that sent the classroom into fits of giggles.

The hair and makeup trial lesson wrapped up, and Iguchi and I visited some other departments. I'm sure we attended an orientation as well, yet my head was so full of thoughts of Mike-san that everything went in one ear and out the other.

When I placed my hand on Ichika's forehead, her eyes fluttered open. "Riku...didn't you go to the info session?"

"It's over. I just got back."

Having just woken up, she gazed at me, head still foggy. Her high fever made her eyes pinkish, almost like a rabbit's.

"Still got a fever, huh? I bought you drinks and jelly snacks. Want some?"

"Thanks. My throat's completely parched."

Sitting up, she gulped down one plastic bottle's contents in one go. As she lifted her chin to finish it, I saw beads of sweat glisten on her neck. Her sweat-drenched pajamas didn't look the least bit comfortable. I knew Ichika's closet like the back of my hand, so I grabbed her a change of clothes while she ate the jellies.

I picked out fresh undergarments and soft cotton pajamas as well as a warm compress. She'd spent the whole day sleeping rather than going to see a doctor, but she seemed to be over the worst of her fever.

"I got you some fresh pajamas," I said. "Why don't you get changed?"

"It hurts to move..."

"All that sweat's going to make you clammy. Let me wipe you down."

Ichika obliged dutifully as I helped her undress; she probably didn't have the energy to struggle thanks to her fever. Even when I began wiping her down with the warm towel, she didn't object.

Large drops of sweat dotted her pale flesh. She squeezed her eyes shut as I wiped away the moisture that pooled between her breasts. Maybe the compress felt good against her skin. I wanted to wash her hair too, but it seemed a little soon for her to take a bath.

I was quite familiar with Ichika's body from touching it so often, but I'd never actually taken a good look at it until now. I noticed that her breasts had grown slightly since we'd started becoming intimate.

"Sorry I couldn't go with you today," she murmured.

"Don't worry about it. I ran into Iguchi, and we ended up going around together."

"Oh. So, you weren't all alone?" Ichika smiled, heaving a half-exhausted sigh of relief as she pulled on a t-shirt. I'd offered to wipe off her lower extremities as well, but she'd politely declined.

As I gave her a rough overview of the beauty school's curriculum, she turned her back and began getting dressed, slipping her panties over her dainty ankles. Her t-shirt wasn't long enough to fully cover her shapely butt. I was annoyed at how my eyes seemed automatically drawn to it.

"Do you think Iguchi-san wants to go there too?" she asked.

"No, though she said she's also interested in fashion design. I didn't see anyone else from our school at the info session, either."

"Then it would be all right if you enrolled there, wouldn't it?"

"I haven't made up my mind to go there yet."

I was certainly interested, though. I'd always curled Ichika's hair and styled it in updos. And cutting hair with scissors had been terrifying yet exhilarating. In addition to granting cosmetology licenses, the school offered exams for makeup qualifications, and I could study both hair and makeup in depth there. Maybe I could further accentuate Ichika's charms if I became a licensed beautician.

I ran my fingers through her sweat-drenched hair, which prompted Ichika to suddenly glance backward. "You aren't getting undressed yourself?"

"I'm not interested in seducing someone running a fever."

"That's not what I meant. You're not going to *change*?"

She pulled on her pajama pants, studying me quizzically. Her closet door was still ajar, so I shut it before I helped her back into bed.

"You aren't going to put any makeup on?"

"No." The last time I'd cross-dressed or put makeup on was the night of the post-festival celebration.

"Why'd you stop?" she whined like a sleepy child, nestling into her comforter. "You've still got lots of clothes here. And everyone's coming home late tonight—no one will see you."

"It's fine."

"How come?"

"I don't need to do it anymore," I replied, softly patting her chest in an attempt to lull her to sleep. Her listless condition made it hard for her to stand her ground. "As long as I have you, I'm fine," I added.

I'd decided not to wear women's clothing anymore, but I didn't have the heart to throw away everything I'd stored in Ichika's closet. Still, I visited her room less and less often. We always slept together in my room. It felt wrong to touch her in here, with the pastel comforter and curtains and the dolls surrounding us on all sides.

I could just barely make out the outline of her soft, supple breasts under the comforter. She moaned so sweetly when my tongue teased her nipples, but part of me detested the thought of hearing those sounds in this room.

As she finally drifted off to sleep, I gave her a soft kiss. There was something I hadn't been able to tell her about: meeting Miyake-san at the beauty school. *If only we'd had an opportunity to talk again.*

As soon as Ichika recovered from her cold, it was my turn to come down with a fever. It was clear as day that she'd passed her bug onto me. She'd been fortunate enough to recover over a weekend, but I had to miss school. There was no one around to take care of me, so my only option was to visit the local clinic and see a doctor on my own.

The clinic shared space with a pediatrician's office, so there were a bunch of kids in the waiting room. Only a handful sat peacefully on their mother's laps while the rest ran amok. Their screams rang in my head, loud enough to make you wonder whether the kids were actually sick.

"You all right?" At first, I thought a nurse was talking to me; my fever made me feel as if my head was stuffed with cotton. It was a man peering in my direction, though.

"It might be best if you lie down for a second," he suggested. "I'll get up."

"Thanks, but I'm okay."

The man wore a mask, so I gathered he had a cold too. His hair was tied into a ponytail; it looked like he was in the process of growing it out. His ankles stuck out of his rumpled sweatpants. I met his gaze, and his neatly manicured eyebrows twitched upward.

"Wait. Are you..." he cut himself off.

"Sorry?"

"Never mind." The man shook his head. Because of his mask, I couldn't make out most of his face. Something about his eyes seemed familiar, but I was feverish, so my vision wouldn't focus.

I was still peering at the man, trying to recall where I'd seen him, when a nurse's voice echoed through the waiting room. "Miyake-san. Miyake Atsuhiko-san. Please come to the consultation room."

The man next to me rose to his feet. As he walked away, realization hit me like a ton of bricks. "Mike-san...?" I murmured under my breath. Apparently, I was audible; *he*—Mike-san—smiled wryly as he glanced back in my direction.

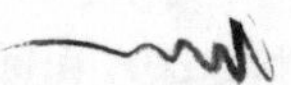

By the time my appointment finished, there was no sign of Mike-san in the waiting room. I picked up my prescription at the front counter and made my way to the local pharmacy, which was crawling with people. Turning in my prescription, I received a number virtually eons from the one currently displayed on the monitor. I was mentally preparing for the long wait ahead when I felt a light tap on my shoulder.

I turned around to see Mike-san. "You're Tono-kun from the information session, right?"

I confirmed this, and Mike-san furrowed his brow as if contemplating something. He'd brought two cups of water from the cooler, so he handed me one, and we sat together on a bench. As he pulled down his mask to take a gulp from his cup, I got a better look at his profile. His Adam's apple bobbed as he swallowed.

When he noticed me looking at him, Mike-san raised his palm to cover his face. "I'm a little embarrassed when people see me without makeup on."

I quickly apologized and averted my gaze.

"I never thought we'd meet in a place like this," he chuckled softly.

"Sorry. I just happened to recognize you."

"Don't worry. I struck up our conversation in the first place."

The sweatsuit-clad version of Mike-san had a low, gravelly voice. I was sure that was partially due to his cold, but obviously, he'd been adopting a feminine tone at the school. Maybe he was so worn out from fever that he lacked the energy to worry about how he sounded.

Mike-san was male. I'd picked up on it during the information session—I'm sure most of the attendees had—but no one had said anything. He'd worn a wig and makeup and dressed in women's clothing, including a skirt and heels, but the veins that bulged at his collar and the muscular calves peeking out below his skirt spoke to the body he'd been born with. And although makeup made his well-defined features gorgeous, his face lacked the soft roundness of a girl's.

My jaw had nearly dropped to the floor when I saw him dressed like that. He reminded me a lot of myself when I wore makeup—maybe because we wore a similar wig style.

"I wanted to hear more about your cross-dressing café," Mike-san told me. "City schools sure are something, huh?"

The corners of his eyes creased as he smiled; I recalled noticing the same catlike expression during the info session. "City schools? Are you not from around here?"

"Nope. I grew up in the middle of nowhere."

People from all over Hokkaido gathered in Sapporo. It was particularly common for young people to flock here to attend vocational schools and universities. Mike-san wasn't even from Hokkaido, though. He was originally from a town in Honshu, across the Tsugaru Strait.

"Why'd you come all the way to Hokkaido?"

The beauty school he attended covered a wide range of subjects, but vocational schools with similar curricula were located throughout Japan, and it wasn't like Mike-san's school had special classes or famous instructors. If the school had a valuable reputation, I would've understood why he enrolled—that was the case with some Hokkaido University students. To be frank, though, it wasn't the kind of institution that would entice students from across the strait.

"There was no chance of anyone I know seeing me walking around in a skirt," replied Mike-san, who'd apparently given up everything to come here.

Miyake Atsuhiko had been born in one of Honshu's many small towns. His family owned a barbershop, and he told me briefly about how he'd grown up watching his father cut hair.

"As a kid, I always had a buzzcut," he said. "And I had the same style in junior high since I was on the baseball team. I tried to grow it out in high school, but my school was strict. They kept forcing me to cut it short again."

His hair was pulled back in a ponytail not for style, but because he was finally growing it out. He generally wore wigs now, he said, but hoped his own hair would be serviceable one day.

"Did you dress up for your class's café, Tono-kun?"

"No. That kind of stuff isn't for me." Lying about my former hobby was second nature.

Mike-san just grinned. "I see." He studied my face. I got the feeling he wanted to say something like, "It would probably look good on you," but he managed to swallow his opinion.

"The first time I wore a skirt was at my high school culture festival," he told me. "It was for a baseball team presentation. I borrowed a girl's uniform and danced around onstage."

All he'd done was switch his uniform for a girl's—he hadn't worn a wig or any makeup. He smiled bitterly as he added that he hadn't shaved his legs or anything, either. Even I could envision the crudeness of the scene.

"But at that moment," he told me, "I realized that was what I'd wanted my whole life."

"Your whole life...?" I echoed.

"As a kid, I somehow got it into my head that, when I grew up, my penis would vanish, and I'd grow breasts." Mike-san reclined on the couch, looking up at the ceiling. "After that performance, I started looking into ways to become a girl. I bought women's clothing and makeup online, but I couldn't try any of it on. I lived in a small town, and it would've caused my family a lot of grief if rumors that their son was 'queer' went around, so I had to keep everything under wraps until I graduated from high school."

Mike-san's voice was almost a hoarse whisper from his—no, her—fever. She told me she'd originally planned to train as a barber and take over her father's shop, explaining how hard it had been to convince her parents to let her attend beauty school instead. It was a common misconception that barbers and hairstylists did the same work, but really, their jobs were completely different.

"I only started dressing as a woman and wearing makeup after I moved here. I'm still not great at it. The girls at school practically mob me trying to give me pointers."

"Aren't you scared of what other people think when they see you...?"

"Of course I'm scared." Mike-san stroked her underarm uncomfortably. Her parents were paying her tuition, but she wasn't getting any money from them beyond that. To support herself, she worked jobs that required physical labor. Even through her sweatshirt, I could tell how muscular she was.

"I got teased for dressing like a girl at that school festival until I graduated. These days, drag queens are on TV more often, but people still look gobsmacked when they see a man cross-dress in real life. I always used to change into women's clothing after getting to school, but now I'm comfortable leaving the house in it. I'm scared of what people think," she concluded, gaze still trained straight ahead, "but I'm more afraid of hiding who I truly am."

There was nothing I could say to her. We sat there in silence until the pharmacist called her to get her prescription.

After getting over my cold and returning to school, one of the first things I did was visit the art room—a place I'd never been before. The moment the door opened, the odor of oil paints filled my nostrils—it didn't smell good at all.

Still, Ichika's eyes practically sparkled as she took in the classroom. "Wow!" she gushed. "Look at all the paintings."

I spotted a row of canvases in different stages of completion. Practically no art club members were visiting the room during lunch; however, Iguchi stood by the window. When she noticed our presence, she turned her head toward us.

"I said don't move, Iguchi," Chiaki told her, his voice exasperated.

"But we have company."

Until that point, Chiaki hadn't even realized Ichika and I were there. I could tell from his severe gaze that he'd been deeply focused. "Wow, Riku. You never come in here. What's up?" he asked, his face softening into a smile.

"I was looking for Iguchi. We heard she'd be in here."

Iguchi's eyes widened in surprise. "You were looking for me?"

I promptly handed over a single postcard.

She glanced at it for a moment, then murmured in recognition, "This is from that beauty school we visited the other day."

"Mike-san said they'd hold their school festival soon, so we should go check it out." She and I had exchanged contact information the day we met at the clinic, and we'd kept in touch since, texting from time to time.

The school festival was a venue for the beauty school students to showcase their new skills, and they planned to hold a joint fashion show with their fashion-design sister school.

Chiaki peeked at the postcard Iguchi held. "Are people only allowed to attend if they've got an invitation?"

"Nope. Ichika's coming too. Mike-san said we're welcome to bring any friends who are interested." Actually, she'd asked me to invite as many people as possible.

Iguchi and I were discussing when to meet up when I noticed that Ichika had disappeared from my side.

"Ichika?"

She was gazing at Chiaki's competition piece, which hung on the wall. It was a landscape painting almost as detailed as a real photo. Then, seeing the painting of the calico cat Chiaki had presented during the send-off event, she seemed to die of cuteness overload.

I took the opportunity to steal a glance at the new project Chiaki was working on, although I didn't know much about oil paintings. It was a portrait that included a large full moon. The figure in the painting was completely nude, and silvery moonlight glinted off their hair.

I could tell at a glance that Iguchi had modeled for this piece. *Those two must be really close if she's acting as Chiaki's nude model.* He'd only painted the tone of the figure's skin, however—no other specific details.

"Is that figure male or female?" As I looked at painting, I'd suddenly been struck with the urge to ask.

"Huh? It's a girl, isn't it?" Ichika said, as if stating the obvious. Given who was modeling, that did seem to be the obvious answer.

Chiaki whistled. He seemed impressed that I'd observed some incongruity. "I didn't expect anyone to wonder."

"The chest was a little smaller than I anticipated."

"Well, excuse me!" Iguchi snapped haughtily, prompting Chiaki to convulse with laughter.

"And the figure's build is different," I added. "It almost lacks softness." Iguchi was tall and statuesque, with broad shoulders, but there were too many discrepancies for the subject of the painting to be her.

"Oh, now that you mention it, I can see it," Ichika agreed. "Don't women have defined waists because they have one rib fewer than men?"

"It's not that they have fewer ribs. Their skeletal structure's just different," Chiaki said. "Men have a wider chest cavity, and women's ribs get smaller as you go down the ribcage." He pointed out the areas with his paintbrush handle. "On the other hand, the female pelvis is broader, while the male's is narrow. Women's waists are more defined due to their skeleton."

It went without saying that most viewers would assume the person in the painting was female. Perhaps Chiaki was happy someone had detected his true intention in the piece; he continued describing differences between the male and female forms.

"Men have broader shoulders because their collarbones are longer. And since male and female pelvises are different widths, the leg bones are obviously different as well. How'd you figure that out, though, Riku?"

"I just...didn't think that looked like Ichika's body."

The words slipped out innocently enough, but Ichika's face turned red as a ripe tomato. Seeing that, Chiaki and Iguchi clasped their own cheeks, exclaiming, "Oh my gosh!" in unison.

While nursing Ichika, I'd taken off her clothes to wipe her sweat. I'd seen then just how different our bodies had become. As children, boys and girls looked similar, but Ichika's form was undoubtedly feminine now.

And, just as she'd changed, so had I. It wasn't only that I'd grown taller. My voice had lowered, and my Adam's apple protruded. The shoulders and waists of women's clothing had gotten too tight, yet the garments bagged awkwardly around my chest and butt. I knew men wound up with angular bodies that gained muscle quickly, but I'd never realized their skeletons were different.

There was no way I'd ever have a body like Ichika's. On the contrary, we'd probably keep getting even more physically different.

"Do you plan to make that figure male or female in the end?" I asked Chiaki.

"I haven't decided yet. Part of me wants to keep it as-is," he replied, eyes trailing over the unfinished painting. "If I was trying to win a competition prize, I'd have to decide, but I'm painting this as I please—it doesn't need to be a man or woman."

I sensed that some element of this painting was occupying his thoughts. A quick glance in Iguchi's direction revealed that it was now *her* turn to blush. Something we weren't privy to seemed to be going on between her and Chiaki.

"We should get going, Ichika."

"Huh?"

There was still some time before our lunch break ended. I knew Ichika wanted to look at the paintings a little longer, but I took her hand, and we left the art room together. When the door closed behind us, I peeked back through the window. Chiaki had noticed Iguchi crying and was wiping away her tears.

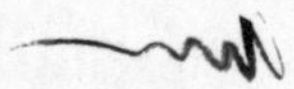

From the day I'd transferred all my belongings to Ichika's room, my own room had appeared to belong to a completely different person. My curtains and bedspread were gray, and my desk was made of drab wood. My bookshelf was mostly full of hand-me-down manga and sports magazines my brothers didn't want anymore. I wasn't fond of my school bag or any of my writing utensils, so when I got home, I just plopped my bag someplace on the floor and ignored it.

My closet wasn't full of clothes, unlike Ichika's. It was where I hid the dirty books my meddlesome big brother pushed on me since I couldn't throw them away. Overall, the space looked just like the stereotypical high school boy's room—exactly as I intended it to.

Recently, though, there was a secret new addition in my room. I removed the item from the depths of the clothing bin where I'd hidden it, then held it up to myself, looking in the mirror. It had gotten a little wrinkled, but there was no way I could hang it in the closet. I never knew when a family member might peek inside, and no one could find out about this—ever.

Still, I just didn't have the heart to toss out the white cocktail dress made as my costume for our class café. I could've taken it to Ichika's room, like so many of my possessions. Even if I had, though, I never would've worn it again. I'd decided not to be the "other me" anymore.

The mirror reflected my bare face. As I draped the dress over my body, something looked unmistakably off. My male classmates had flaunted that incongruity at the festival café, acting as if it were plain as day, but the thought of doing likewise disgusted me to the core.

I'd grown taller over summer break, and although I hadn't been exercising, I felt more muscular. My facial hair was coming in thicker too. I was all too aware of my body becoming more and more masculine.

At this point, makeup could still hide it, and there were still women's clothes that flattered me. But the day when I couldn't conceal my male traits anymore would likely come soon. However hard I wished for an androgynous body—like the one in Chiaki's portrait—that wasn't in the cards for me.

"Riku? Are you back yet?" Someone knocked lightly on the door to my room. I hurriedly shut my closet. "It's about the beauty school festival."

The radiance of a single flower brightened my room's masculine squalor as Ichika walked in. We'd only walked home from school separately, but I felt like I hadn't seen her all day. She was in the middle of saying something, but I darted over and pulled her petite frame into a tight embrace.

"Riku? What's going on?"

"Just let me stay like this." I buried my face in her hair, breathing in her scent. My hands moved to her butt automatically.

She pinched me hard. "That can wait until I'm done talking."

"Sorry..."

"I'm not going to make it to the beauty school festival," she informed me. "Should I contact someone to tell them I can't go?"

I doubted it would be necessary, but Ichika was earnest like that. When I said I'd notify Mike-san, she grinned and thanked me. Her expression was so cute that I just wanted to gobble her up.

"Sorry," she added. "Something came up that day."

"It's fine. Chiaki and Iguchi are coming. If those two are there, I'm sure Mike-san will be happy."

"I wanted to meet Mike-san too, though," Ichika said wistfully.

I hadn't gone into too much detail about Mike-san with Ichika. I'd just told her I'd met someone who gave me lots of information about the beauty school. I hadn't said anything about Mike-san being physically male but identifying as a woman. Telling someone else's secret casually would be outing them. Although Mike-san had talked about herself openly, I still felt it'd be wrong to broach the topic with someone she'd never met.

"It'd be interesting to meet someone catlike," Ichika added. "That's how you described Mike-san, right?"

"Yeah...I'd say there's a slight feline resemblance."

"Mike" was short for her surname, Miyake. It was just a shot in the dark, but I figured she probably didn't like being referred to by her given name.

I glanced over at my closet, Ichika still in my arms. Closet—the same word used to describe the space where people stored clothes also described the location of someone concealing a secret in their heart. My dress was hidden in the closet—just like me. Only Ichika knew my secret.

After I suddenly went quiet, Ichika peered into my face. "Riku...?" Even after I leaned down to kiss her, her worried expression remained. "Did something happen?"

"It's nothing," I smiled, trying to smooth things over by squishing my cheek against hers, like I used to with my teddy bear.

"So, yeah, one of the friends I planned to bring can't make it," I told Mike-san over the phone.

"No problem. It's not like we had seats reserved or anything. Thanks for letting me know, though." A single sneeze accompanied Mike-san's response.

I could still hear her sniffling as I asked if she was okay.

"I've been so busy lately prepping for the school festival, I haven't had much time to rest. My voice is all nasal now. It's so embarrassing."

"Sorry to make you talk on the phone. Are your preparations going smoothly?"

"Well, it's been nearly impossible to settle on a cohesive concept," she sighed. "None of the higher-ups on any course want to budge. It's just one new take after another."

For the festival's fashion show, students from the beauty school's hair and makeup department, nail art department, and fashion department—as well as from the sister school for fashion design—would team up to deck out models head to toe. The models were studying at the school too. The students themselves would be responsible for everything, even setting up the venue. And although the fashion show was part of the school festival, the results would likely influence their grades.

"Various industry members come watch, so everyone wants to show off their best work," Mike-san explained. "We're also marked, and if a model's hair and makeup score high enough, we get invitations to enter contests and stuff. So I have to do whatever it takes."

She'd gotten sick in the first place because she was so busy with meetings that ran late day after day, followed by shifts at her part-time job. She'd had no time to rest or recover from her fatigue, and since she lived alone, no one was around to look after her. All she could do was wait for her fever to break, unable to eat or drink anything.

"Couldn't you have asked a friend to come take care of you?"

"Wouldn't it be awkward asking a female friend to swing by a guy's house as a favor? On the other hand, I don't want men coming to my place either."

I didn't know what to say to that.

The line remained silent until Mike-san spoke up. "So," she continued cheerfully, "I'm guessing the fact that you called means there's something else you want to talk about?"

"Um, Mike-san..."

"Yes?"

"I love my girlfriend."

"You suddenly felt the need to brag about that?" She giggled over the line.

I chuckled in response, stroking Ichika's head as she slept in my bed. Once Ichika was off to dreamland, basically nothing roused her. I confirmed that she was breathing rhythmically, then searched for the words I wanted to say.

"What is it?" Mike-san asked. "Did you fight?"

"Nope. We're affectionate every day."

What on earth am I building up to? I let my gaze wander until it rested on Ichika's bag, which she'd placed under my bed. I never should've gone through it without permission, even if it *was* just to check her homework notebook. I didn't want anyone opening my closet door; Ichika, likewise, would obviously have a secret or two she wanted to conceal.

In her bag, I'd seen more brochures and pamphlets for info sessions, mostly for beauty schools and so on. One brochure was a little different, though—it advertised an info session for a women's junior college scheduled on the same day as Mike-san's school festival. Realizing that Ichika had canceled her plans with me to visit that school completely threw me for a loop.

"I love my girlfriend," I repeated.

"Yes, you've made that very clear."

"I think I depend on her too much, though." *Why was she planning to go without saying anything? She could at least have mentioned it to me.*

I knew Ichika and I wouldn't be together 24/7 once high school ended, and it wasn't like we'd promised to attend the same school after graduating. She still hadn't decided what she wanted to do, and it wasn't at all strange that another institution might've caught her eye. Yet when I spotted that pamphlet, I couldn't help thinking, *Maybe Ichika wants to get away from me.*

Since we were children, all she'd done was protect me. I was self-aware enough to realize how audacious my behavior had become after I started hanging out in her room, but I'd almost taken her indulgence for granted, since she never rebuffed me.

I loved Ichika. I wanted to kiss her, to hold her. On the other hand, part of me seethed with jealously at her femininity.

It wasn't that I wanted to be a girl myself. She was just so precious and lovely that I couldn't bear it. However hard I racked my brain, I couldn't figure out what I wanted to do with myself.

"I...might be holding her back," I continued.

My possessiveness had bound her hand and foot. I'd started to assume she'd always be by my side; I even felt assured that she'd accommodate my career. I'd tried to shove her into my closet to protect myself without considering, for one moment, how she felt.

The date of the beauty school festival finally arrived. As Ichika got ready for her own excursion, she asked me to help with her makeup.

"It never turns out well when I do it myself," she told me. "When it comes to these kinds of things, you're the best, hands down, Riku."

I had to admit, it felt nice to be needed. I headed to her room for the first time in a while and helped her coordinate a head-to-toe look. She didn't offer any information on her destination, but since she was visiting a women's college, she was likely aware that many students would dress stylishly.

I'd applied Ichika's makeup so many times that I could've done it with my eyes shut. We didn't have much time before she needed to leave, so I couldn't make it too fancy, but she smiled in satisfaction at the mirror once I finished.

"You outdid yourself again, Riku! My hair's super cute too."

"The wind's strong today, so I styled it in an updo."

Even since Mike-san showed us how to do that dumpling-style bun, I'd been dying to try it out. My lips moved instinctively to kiss the exposed nape of Ichika's neck when it peeked out from under her pulled-up hair.

"Thanks so much," she said. "Sorry to ask for help when you're getting ready to go out yourself."

"I'm not in that much of a rush. Mike-san's show isn't until this afternoon. But you'll miss the subway if you don't head out soon!"

Ichika shrieked as she glanced back into the mirror. As she hurriedly departed, I saw her off, then finished getting ready myself and made my way to the station. The beauty school and the junior college Ichika was visiting were on the same train line, but they were in opposite directions, so there was no point in us leaving together.

Iguchi and Chiaki had apparently met up before the festival. By the time I arrived, they'd entered the venue and were checking out the exhibits with great interest. I didn't think Chiaki was interested in beauty, but he seemed practically entranced by a series of images of body art. Maybe there was a strong link between fine art and beauty.

Mike-san's show wouldn't start until the afternoon, but other shows were taking place in the morning. Students from the modeling course showed off the results of their practice, gliding down the runway effortlessly. High heels exaggerated their already-tall silhouettes, and their walks were carefully rehearsed to flatter the clothes they wore. It was impossible not to be drawn in by their long, shapely legs.

Some students were styling a mannequin's hair within a specific time limit while others showed off competing makeup looks. Regardless of the challenge, everyone looked deadly serious. At the end of each show, the participating students lined up on stage to receive feedback from instructors and special guests. Some of the criticism was harsh; several students burst into tears. But that was the reality of trying to go professional.

As soon as I arrived, I'd contacted Mike-san to ask if we could go behind the scenes during her show. It was taking her a while to get back to me, so I assumed she was busy getting everything ready.

There were no refreshment booths inside the school, so we decided to get snacks from the food trucks outside. I could see Sapporo TV Tower from here. It looked even larger than it did from our high school. Both schools were near downtown Sapporo, and it seemed amazing that a small change of location could produce a completely different atmosphere at the two institutions.

As I let that revelation wash over me, Mike-san finally called me. "Where are you now, Tono-kun?"

"Near the food trucks. Iguchi's waiting in line for a crepe."

"Got it. I'll be right there."

Mike-san reached the food trucks soon after our brief phone call. She waved when she saw us. As Iguchi took in Mike-san's appearance, she stood stock-still, completely forgetting to move forward in the crepe line.

"Thanks for coming today," Mike-san said. "Are you having fun at the festival so far?"

"Yes!" I replied. "And it's been really informative."

"I wanted to take you guys backstage so you could see us get ready, but everyone's a bit on edge at the moment. I'm sure you can talk to them after the show, though."

"Mike-san, that outfit..." I trailed off.

Mike-san glanced down at herself. "Oh, this? Is it weird?"

"It...looks great on you."

Mike-san was dressed in a man's suit. She wasn't wearing makeup, and her half-grown-out hair was tied back simply. Something about the dark-gray suit and violet shirt she wore enhanced the casual hairstyle's charm.

Iguchi and Chiaki gushed excitedly. "You look so cool!"

"That's totally sexy!"

"I suddenly ended up becoming a model," Mike-san responded with a breezy smile. "I think this's the first time I've worn a suit since the school's entrance ceremony."

The suit was apparently a fashion school student's masterpiece. The original model had come down with a cold, and Mike-san's body type was the most similar, so filling in fell to her.

"Will you change back into your usual style for your own show?"

"I can't! Our show starts as soon as this one's over. Besides, I'd rather spend any spare time getting our model ready."

"Could you get changed in time for the instructors' evaluations...?"

"Probably not. This all went down just last night. The designer pulled an all-nighter to resize the suit for me, and I stayed to help her out. The only clothes I have with me are basically loungewear. There's no way I could show up in front of teachers wearing that."

To make the finish line for the school festival, she hadn't been able to afford to worry about her appearance. She hadn't even had time to bathe.

"You probably shouldn't get too close to me," she added, trying to keep her distance.

Her appearance made my chest feel excruciatingly tight. "Weren't there plenty of boys who could model? Why'd it have to be you...?"

"If I didn't do it, the girl who worked so hard to make this suit would be docked a lot of points."

"But..."

Mike-san sighed, smiling weakly at my stubbornness. "You've heard of calico cats, right, Tono-kun?"

The sudden change in subject confused me so much, all I could do was nod.

"They're usually female, because of a recessive gene," Mike-san continued. "Male kittens are very uncommon. I'm sure you learned about calico cats at school."

She meant in biology class. We'd actually studied the genetics behind red-green colorblindness at school. The gene for colorblindness was part of the X chromosome. Men had XY chromosomes, while women had XX chromosomes. For a woman to be colorblind, she needed a genetic abnormality on both X chromosomes, but men always ended up colorblind if they received an X chromosome from a mother with the genetic abnormality. That was why colorblindness was relatively common in men.

The same principles applied to calico cats. Mike-san was only one year out of high school, and she'd read about calico genetics in her biology textbook. "I can't imagine how traumatic things must be for male calicos," she continued. "It's just them. All the other calicos are female. They can't change their bodies, and they don't blend in with other tomcats. I'm sure the opposite situation occurs in humans too—you know, being born in a female body, but identifying as male."

"Mike-san..."

"I've been a calico all along, so this is no big sacrifice. Anyway, it's almost time," she added, checking her watch before turning to head back inside.

As I watched her walk away, I felt utterly helpless. All I could do was clench my fists.

The first presentation of the afternoon was a show featuring men's suits created by first-year fashion school students. They'd all used the same pattern, but each suit's fabric was unique. Garments by students whose work wasn't in the show were simply displayed on mannequins, but the suits coming down the runway were tailored to fit the student models perfectly—after all, fit would be a critical factor in the instructors' evaluations.

When we returned to the auditorium where the shows were staged, we found it full of way more spectators than that morning. We'd gotten back late, and there was only standing room left. I leaned against the wall as I waited for Mike-san's turn. I was still disgruntled about her situation; frankly, I didn't want to see her forced to walk the runway in a suit, but it felt wrong to abandon her. There was conviction in her decision to appear before us dressed like that.

After the first few suits, it was finally Mike-san's turn to stride onstage. A cheer went up from the students. Some yelled "Mike!" in support—they were probably well aware of her usual appearance. Mike-san smiled in response, walking the runway with her shoulders pulled back and her head held high. Seeing her immediately took me back to junior high.

After my classmates found out I dressed like a girl, I desperately practiced looking and acting as masculine as possible. I stopped walking pigeon-toed and began to strut casually with a hand stuck into my pocket. The night after I cut my hair, I wept secretly in bed. It took every ounce of strength to withstand the pain of, say, replacing my pencil case or removing the keychains from my school bag.

I was in front of my apartment complex's trash room, about to dispose of the teddy bear I cuddled every night, when Ichika appeared.

"Are you throwing that away?" she asked when she spotted me locked in place. "You love that teddy bear, Riku. Why get rid of him?"

"People call me gay because I have stuff like this."

I was desperately trying to snuff out every trace of girlishness in my room, but I just couldn't bring myself to get rid of my teddy bear. He was my beloved partner; I couldn't sleep without him. I'd cuddled him so much over the years, his fur was worn.

"Can I have him, then?" Ichika reached out to take the bear and cradled it. "I've always had my eye on this little guy. Do you mind if *I* sleep with him from now on?"

Ichika had lots of other toys in her room. She kept some stuffed animals arranged in front of her pillow. They were in much better shape than mine and were made of softer material. The thought of adding my shabby teddy bear to the mix made me pause.

"You can come to my room and see him anytime you want, okay?"

When Ichika said that, the true meaning of her actions finally dawned on me. She was the only one who saw up-close how hard I was attempting to blend in at school. She was trying to protect me so I wouldn't lose everything precious to me.

Funnily enough, even without my teddy bear, I wasn't scared at night. I slept tight in comfort, knowing Ichika was cuddling the bear in the apartment next door, in a room with the exact same layout as mine.

All Ichika had ever done was protect me.

After we watched Mike-san walk the runway and leave the stage, I stepped away from the wall. "Sorry, Iguchi. I gotta head out for a bit."

"Why? Mike-san's show is coming up."

"I'll make it back as soon as I can."

As I stepped out of the dark auditorium, the outdoor light dazzled me. The fashion show's pounding music still thumped euphorically in my head, and I dashed toward the subway station as though the beat was propelling me. By the time I'd gone home and returned, Mike's show would probably be over. The evaluation might be done too. Every minute—every *second*—mattered.

I was in such a rush that my phone slipped out of my pocket and hit the ground. The impact cracked the screen, but I didn't have the luxury of time to be upset. When I checked to see if it still worked, I noticed Ichika had sent a single text.

"My thing finished up, so I'm heading to the festival now. Hopefully I'll be in time for the show."

The junior college she'd visited was in the opposite direction from the beauty school. To get to the show, she'd have to pass the station closest to our apartment complex. When I checked the time stamp on the text, I realized it hadn't been too long since she messaged me.

I hurriedly dialed her number but couldn't get through. If she was on the subway, she might not pick up. I felt too flustered to text, though, so I tried calling again and again.

"Hello? Riku?"

"Where are you right now, Ichika?" I practically screamed.

In contrast, Ichika's voice was hushed. She was probably trying to conceal the fact she had answered her phone after noticing my unusual barrage of missed calls. "On the subway, at the station by our house. It'll still be a while until I get there."

"You need to get off that train and go home!"

Perhaps the fierceness of my demand surprised her. The sound of the train pulling away a few seconds later told me she'd responded instinctively and disembarked at our local station.

"Stop by my apartment," I continued. "I need you to bring something over."

"Got it. Did you forget something?" She asked where it was.

I heaved an internal sigh of relief that I hadn't hidden the item in her room. It would've taken much longer to find there. "It's in my closet. At the bottom of the clothing bin in the very back."

"What should I take out?"

I always depended on Ichika. Someday, I'd have to make it up to her.

"My white cocktail dress from our school festival."

If I showed someone else the same kindness Ichika treated me with, could I finally get past always acting like a spoiled child?

After I met up with Ichika, Iguchi and Chiaki brought us to the fashion show's green room. I'd missed seeing Mike-san's group, but some other students were still presenting designs. The proceedings were taking a little longer than expected, so there'd probably be some downtime before evaluations started.

I opened the green room door so forcefully that everyone turned to stare. Ichika and I were covered in sweat after our mad dash, which garnered some questioning looks.

Someone called to me from the back. "Tono-kun? What's going on?"

The voice came from Mike-san's group. Mike-san's model was among them, but I didn't have the mental capacity to admire her outfit. Charging straight into the green room, I forced the paper bag I was carrying into Mike-san's arms.

"Put this on!"

"What is it?"

"A dress. It's white. It won't be as well-tailored as the suit, but it's something." I was panting so hard, I barely got the words out.

Ichika was also completely winded, and she still had no clue what was going on.

Mike-san pulled the dress from the bag. She sighed softly as she gazed down at it. "It's very pretty...but I'm sure it won't fit me."

"It will. Because it's mine."

I felt her group's eyes pierce me, but I paid them no heed. "We have similar body types," I continued. "Your shoulders might be a little noticeable if you just wear the dress, but if you cover them with a shawl or something, it should be fine. And if you wear a wig, you can style it to distract from your Adam's apple."

"How do you know so much about all this?" Mike-san asked.

Iguchi and Chiaki watched our exchange; their gazes burned. I clenched my fists, hoping to shake my discomfort. "I wore women's clothes too for a long time."

But even when I found feminine clothing that I liked, it was becoming less likely that it would fit right. Sure, I could force myself into a garment, but my frame usually neutralized the design's strengths. Without breasts, I lacked a beautifully curved silhouette, and low necklines emphasized my Adam's apple. I'd gradually started researching clothing combinations that still suited me, and makeup styles that made me look more feminine.

"My evaluation's going to start soon," Mike said uncertainly.

A group member piped up from the sidelines. "Do it, Mike! If we divvy up the work, we can get you ready in time. We've got wigs and makeup here. It should be fine."

I figured she was in the hair and makeup department, as she started applying primer to Mike-san's face before Mike-san even had a chance to respond. A girl with silk flowers in her hair began trimming the ends of a wig with scissors.

Soon, all the eyes in the green room were glued on us. If we ran out of any of the cosmetics on hand, all we'd have to do was yell and someone would lend us more. Mike-san just sat there as everyone worked on her.

"Um..." I interjected.

"Yes?" said one of the students making her up.

"She has defined cheekbones. You should soften them with blush and highlighter."

"Tell us something we don't know. Who do you think taught her to do makeup in the first place?!"

I'd never felt such relief after a reprimand. Realizing that my presence wasn't vital, I slumped on the floor next to Ichika. Mike-san went behind a curtain to put on the dress so her classmates could complete the finishing touches. Everyone waited eagerly for her to come out.

Instead, she whispered feebly from beyond the thin curtain. "I can't do it. Not in this dress."

"It's fine! Just come out already!"

She didn't respond, so someone pulled the curtain and exposed Mike-san, who had her arms wrapped around herself as if concealing her appearance. Mike-san and I *were* about the same height, but she was way more muscular. Her rounded biceps bulged, and the leg peeking from the dress's slit was defined with deep, sinewy lines. The dress did fit her, but as it was, she wouldn't want to wear it.

The costumes for our class's cross-dressing café had been inspired by drag queens. If Mike-san styled herself accordingly, that might reduce some of the outfit's awkwardness. It wouldn't accord with how she felt about herself, though.

Her group members offered different suggestions—she could draw attention from the dress with a voluminous hairstyle or wear dark stockings—but none seemed to do the trick.

"Sorry, everyone. I've had enough..." Mike-san trailed off in a barely audible voice, wilting from embarrassment.

She glanced around for makeup remover. All we could do was look on in frustration, everyone thinking that same thing: *Can we do anything for her?*

We were still at a loss when a single voice piped up somewhere in the green room. "Could I alter that dress?"

"It...doesn't belong to me."

"No problem!" I shouted. "Do whatever you want with it!"

At that, a petite girl barreled across the crowded room in our direction. "I need some designers to help me! Bring any leftover fabric you can find over here!"

Scissors in hand, she sliced through the hem of the dress, cutting several openings the length of the original slit. Several girls formed a human wall around the deeply flushed Mike-san to hide her exposed legs.

"I'm so sorry I made you wear a suit, Mike," the petite girl added. "I'm sure you didn't feel comfortable."

I gathered she'd made the suit Mike-san wore earlier. The corners of her eyes were full of tears; she wiped them away, then began stitching scavenged fabric into the new slits she'd cut in the garment. It had started as a sateen cocktail dress, but the additional fabric transformed its simple shape into something much more elegant.

The girl intentionally left the hem uneven, which exposed Mike-san's ankle and made her look more slender and delicate. For the most part, she'd only added white fabric, but she'd used flower print exquisitely to create several key accents, boosting the dress from beautiful to gorgeous.

The design students worked without hesitation. They didn't discuss what they were going to do ahead of time, yet they all seemed focused on the same vision.

"How much time is left? We still need to cover her neck!"

"We can't leave her shoulders bare either. We gotta cover them."

"Anyone have a scarf?"

People chimed in right and left. The girl who'd made the suit was hand-sewing Mike-san's hem at top speed. The fabric she'd added made the dress roomier, creating a soft curve below the waist.

"She doesn't need a scarf," a male student yelled from one corner. "You'll only call attention to that area if you go out of your way to cover it. Just create volume by layering organdy around the neckline. Catching the eye with something else is a better approach. You can use our group's necklace, if you want."

There was a brief, awkward pause as he approached the all-female team working on Mike-san, but the newcomer seemed completely undaunted as he handed over the accessory.

"You need to be confident, Miyake," he added. "Slouching makes your whole body look off-balance. Stick your chest out and stand up proud."

His encouragement spurred the other students to action.

"Cinch this ribbon around her stomach! It'll define her waist!"

"Her arms might look more delicate with a bracelet or two!"

"I have big feet, so you can probably wear my high heels!"

In what seemed like the blink of an eye, Mike-san was made up and dressed to the nines. A group of design students split up to finish mending the sliced skirt until it was good as new. One was particularly annoyed with the messy sewing; she muttered complaints as she fixed the seams.

After curling Mike-san's wig with an iron for a softer appearance, the group began the final makeup touchups.

"Come on, Mike, don't cry. Your makeup will run."

"Sorry, but I..."

"You can cry as much as you want once everything's over. Just hang on a little longer."

Mike-san looked at the ceiling, holding back her tears at the show of support. When she realized someone was trying to apply her blush, she forced a smile to show them the apples of her cheeks. The grin was awkward, but she looked adorable.

After the beauty school festival, it was getting dark. You could almost hear winter's footsteps approaching as the sun spent less time in the sky with each passing day. Ichika and I parted with Iguchi and Chiaki at the subway station and headed home.

As we approached the park, Ichika squeezed my hand. "Mind if we pause here for a bit?"

It was after sunset, so no children were frolicking there, and streetlamps cast a dim glow on the playground equipment. Ichika headed straight for the jungle gym where I'd always used to hide, but didn't go inside it. Instead, we scaled the ladder, clambered to the top, and sat on the roof. Ichika had been a high-spirited child; back in the day, this was one of her favorite places.

"That school festival was fun, huh?" she remarked.

"Yeah, it was."

"Mike-san looked stunning."

The beauty school students had finished getting her ready just before the evaluations began. My classmates and I had left the green room and returned to the auditorium, sitting in the audience to watch. Iguchi and Chiaki had heard me come out, but they didn't say a word about it the entire time.

Mike-san stood onstage in her white dress, her fully styled hair, makeup, and accessories transforming her into the picture of sophistication. The instructors praised the easy-to-grasp concept of the look her group had presented, lauding each department's success in carrying out their duties. The evaluation also pointed out one flaw after another, but you could tell the critiques were tough love.

After the instructors gave their remarks, it was a guest judge's turn to take the microphone. They seemed to remember Mike-san from earlier. "If I recall correctly, you modeled a suit on the runway earlier. I'm impressed you could change your look so quickly. Did you do that on your own?"

"No. Everyone helped me get ready." It wasn't just her group who'd lent her a hand. All the students present had played a part.

"I feel like I've had the chance to see two assignments from your team. You executed both very well."

Mike-san's group bowed their heads appreciatively at the compliment, and the auditorium filled with applause.

"You didn't end up getting rid of that dress, huh, Riku?" Ichika asked.

Her question brought me back to the present. "No, but I can't wear it now. It got all chopped up."

I looked at the sky. The stars appeared even closer from here, and the adrenaline from the fashion show lingered within me. Taking a deep breath, I revealed the desire bubbling in my heart. "I'd like to enroll at that school."

"I think it would suit you perfectly."

"Is there someplace you're interested in, Ichika?" I chose my words carefully to avoid revealing that I knew about the junior college.

After a slightly uncomfortable pause, she mustered the courage to tell me, "I went to an info session at a junior college today."

"Oh, yeah?" I said casually, letting her get away with it.

"They have general education and nutrition departments, but what really caught my eye was the early childhood education department."

"You want to teach preschool…?" Never in a million years had I expected her to choose that profession. I'd known Ichika a long time, and she'd never seemed particularly interested in children. I'd seen the ECE department listed on the junior college's pamphlet, but I figured Ichika was interested in general education or something.

"I thought about going to the same school as you, but I wondered if maybe there's something else I can do."

"What do you mean?"

She looked me straight in the eye. "If I'm a preschool teacher, I can let little boys wear skirts, if that's what they want."

Her small hands rested atop mine. They felt chilly from the night air. "If they aren't allowed to do that kind of thing as children, they'll grow up thinking it's taboo. Maybe having one teacher who understands their feelings could ease their worries—even if just a bit."

Ichika and I had been together since childhood. She'd seen firsthand how teachers kept me from wearing skirts, how boys teased me, and how girls treated me with contempt. She'd always been my one and only ally.

"I think you'd be a good teacher, Ichika."

"Then you can leave the kids to me." She squeezed my hand. "You're in charge of the adults, okay? You can teach them what to wear and how to apply makeup."

"Me?"

"You're an avid learner, and you always come up with such smart ideas. I think you'll get even more gorgeous attending that beauty school."

I lifted her hand and brought it to my lips. I could smell the fragrance she'd dabbed on her wrist. It was the same as mine, but it smelled completely different—a womanly perfume. That was something I could never obtain, but I always had it by my side.

"Can I visit your room again, Ichika?"

"Of course. I want you to teach me more about makeup too." She shivered in the evening breeze.

"Just makeup...?" I wrapped my arms around her.

She tensed in surprise for a moment, then leaned into me gently. Even through her clothes, I felt her slender-yet-soft frame. I closed my eyes as I breathed in her scent. The envy I'd always felt toward her seemed to have completely disappeared.

"Ichika?"

"Yeah?"

"You'd make sure to tell me if I didn't look good in makeup or skirts anymore, right?"

From here on, our bodies would continue to diverge. Hers would become more feminine, while mine would grow more masculine. Someday, the clothing I liked wouldn't flatter me. Would she really tell me when that day came?

"What're you talking about?" Ichika gazed up at me from within my embrace. "No matter what you wear, you're always *you*, Riku."

My lips parted to utter her name, but she planted a kiss on them before the word escaped.

"Ichika...please don't ever change, either."

As long as she was by my side, I could just be me—whichever "me" that was. There was no greater comfort than someone accepting you exactly as you were.

I lowered my head as if in prayer to meet her lips once more.

You're my goddess, precious and beloved above all others. My one and only treasure.